THE WORLD-WIDE DESSERT CONTEST

A RICHARD
JACKSON
BOOK

THE WORLD-WIDE

WIDE

ORCHARD BOOKS

A division of Franklin Watts, Inc.

New York and London

DESSERT CONTEST

BY DAN ELISH

Illustrated by John Steven Gurney

Orchard Books, 387 Park Avenue South,
New York, New York 10016

Orchard Books Great Britain, 10 Golden Square,
London W1R 3AF England

Orchard Books Australia, 14 Mars Road, Lane Cove,
New South Wales 2066

Orchard Books Canada, 20 Torbay Road,
Markham, Ontario 23P 1G6

Orchard Books is a division of Franklin Watts, Inc.

Manufactured in the United States of America
Book design by Mina Greenstein
The text of this book is set in 12 pt. Walbaum
10 9 8 7 6 5 4 3 2 1

Library of Congress Cataloging-in-Publication
Elish, Dan
The Worldwide Dessert Contest.
Summary: Gentle John Applefeller enters his trampoline-size
apple pancake against sly Sylvester Sweet's double-chocolate-
fudge-raspberry-coconut-lime swirl in The Worldwide Dessert
Contest. [1. Desserts—Fiction. 2. Contests—Fiction] I. Title.
PZ7.E4257Wo 1988 [Fic] 87-24694
ISBN 0-531-05752-6
ISBN 0-531-08352-7 (lib. bdg.)

For
   my
      grandfather

Acknowledgments

Special thanks to:

John • Billy

Mom • Dave

Mary • Christine • Skip

Bart • Mark • Anne

Meg • Mark

Doug • Nana • Daphne

Nora • John

Susan • Harry • Eloise

Charlie

Wendie

Dad • Madeleine

Jonathan • Marian

Matt

Mark • Allison

Dick • Dan • Julia

Suzanne

Lisa   Betsy

Doug

Lauren • Elly • Chuck

Tom

a

David • Lisa

n

d

Seth

Contents

PART ONE

PART TWO

Contents

PART THREE

Principal Characters

John Applefeller * * * Our hero, an apple dessert chef

Stanley * * * Applefeller's faithful ten-year-old assistant

Aunt Harriet * * * Applefeller's late aunt

Morocco * * * Applefeller's horse

Sylvester S. Sweet * * * A dessert villain

Dentina * * * Sweet's assistant

Tuba * * * Sweet's pet elephant

Judge Nathaniel Barkle * * * Head judge of The Worldwide Dessert Contest

Judge Brewster McLaughlin * * * The fat sugar expert

Judge Hamilton Crusthardy * * * The cake specialist with a powerful jaw

Judge George Saucery * * * The stern and serious ice cream authority

Josiah Benson * * * The Worldwide Dessert Contest janitor

Captain B. Rollie Ragoon * * * A magical apple pie chef

Princess Irma A. Frostina * * * A dessert chef from southern Germany

Reginald Coco and Razine * * * Two dessert chefs from eastern India

Michel Deserts * * * A dessert chef from Paris

PART

ONE

1 · John Applefeller

JOHN APPLEFELLER of Appleton loved desserts.

Especially apple desserts.

He loved eating them, but even more, he loved making them—pies, strudels, crisps, and cakes. As his Aunt Harriet used to say: *If a man truly cares about making desserts, an apple dessert is what he should make.* No one knew how Aunt Harriet had come by such wisdom, but John Applefeller, a man of some forty years, had lived the better part of his life by his aunt's motto.

And now, after a decade of making all kinds of different desserts, John Applefeller had just completed the greatest creation of his career—the world's largest apple pancake.

"This is some dessert! Some dessert, I tell you!" Applefeller said to his ten-year-old assistant, Stanley, who lived with his parents half a mile down the road.

Applefeller and Stanley were standing by seven strong apple trees that grew in front of Applefeller's small red farmhouse. It was early morning.

"Well, it certainly is a new kind of dessert, isn't it, sir?" Stanley said.

3

"No one else could have thought of a dessert so original," Applefeller continued, as they hoisted the apple pancake onto a large brown cart. "This pancake is ten feet wide and three feet thick. I'll be sure to win first prize today in The Worldwide Dessert Contest!"

Applefeller and Stanley were about to leave for the fantastic event. Each year in mid-July all the greatest dessert chefs in the world traveled to Appleton Dessert Stadium to enter this contest, bringing with them delicious concoctions to delight the judges. And the winner of the contest, the creator of the best dessert of the year, received a trophy more precious than gold—the Silver Spoon, a beautiful hand-carved ice cream serving spoon. Dedicated dessert chefs would do nearly anything to possess this cherished prize. In northern Peru, an old woman hobbled halfway around her country with a cane in search of a pumpkin that was big enough and orange enough to use in her pumpkin pie. In India, one chef climbed Mount Everest in search of a rare polar sugarcane to use in his mocha-chip ice cream.

John Applefeller wanted to win the Silver Spoon more than anyone. Nearly every hour of every one of his days was spent in his small kitchen, mixing, tasting, stirring, and baking. But unfortunately, Applefeller had had very bad luck in the contest. He had finished in last place all ten years he had entered—never third to last or even second to last, but always *last*.

This year he knew he would do better.

"If I do say so myself, Stanley," Applefeller said as he spread a giant sheet of wax paper over the pancake, "this pancake is perfect. It's golden brown without being too golden or too brown. And the fluffiness of the pancake is fluffy, though not overly fluffed."

"I couldn't agree more, sir," Stanley said.

Applefeller glanced at his watch.

"But enough of this talk. The contest begins in one hour. We mustn't be late! And as my Aunt Harriet said until her dying day: *When you don't want to be late, being on time makes good sense.*"

Stanley walked into Applefeller's barn and reappeared a minute later leading Applefeller's small pinto horse, Morocco, by her halter. Stanley hitched Morocco to the front of the cart. Then he and Applefeller climbed aboard. Stanley took the reins, and Morocco broke into a trot. After a short ride through the outskirts of Appleton, Morocco turned a wide corner.

Before Applefeller and Stanley, about a mile away, stood Appleton Dessert Stadium, an old-style arena with high bleachers surrounding a large field. In front of the stadium was a large arch decorated with ribbons and streamers and a sign that read: THE WORLDWIDE DESSERT CONTEST. Applefeller and Stanley rode toward the arch and were soon in the thick of a great crowd.

Hundreds and hundreds of people milled about. Buses,

vans, and station wagons carrying excited dessert fans were drawing up in front of the main entrance. Rich men pulled into the parking lot in fancy cars. One man arrived in a Porsche shaped like a giant ice cream cone; another, in a Mercedes Benz painted like a hot fudge sundae. People oohed and aahed as they saw or thought they saw famous movie stars arriving. Policemen roamed freely throughout the crowd answering questions and making sure no fan got out of control as everyone rushed toward the spectators' gate, holding tightly onto their tickets.

And the few remaining tickets were selling like cupcakes.

"Tickets here! Tickets! Real good seats! Field level! See the judges' mouths up close as they chew! Only fifty dollars!" yelled one man.

And vendors swarmed around the area selling desserts. There was a man wearing an enormous banana suit selling banana splits. There was a woman dressed as a giant cocoa bean selling chocolate ice cream. Boys and girls shrieked with delight as they bought sweets from these human confections.

Applefeller and Stanley rode bravely through this whirlwind of honking cars, screaming vendors, and rushing people, making their way toward a side gate marked Contestants. Here they would see the "dessert registrar," the man who checked in every contestant and told them where on the field to set up their tables. But when Applefeller and Stanley were only ten feet from the contestants' gate, a group of dessert fans suddenly recognized Applefeller.

"Hey look! There's John Applefeller!" a teenaged boy cried out. "He's finished in last place for ten years in a row!"

"Yeah!" cried a young woman. "It's incredible that one chef can be so bad!"

"But what's really funny is why he finishes in last place!" said the teenaged boy.

"Why?" asked a little girl.

"You mean you don't know?"

"No!" said the girl.

"Applefeller's desserts aren't really desserts at all!" said the woman. "They change into other things at the last minute!"

"You're joking!"

"No, it's true!" said an older man. "Last year his apple soufflé puffed up into a giant balloon!"

"You're pulling my leg!"

"No, he's not!" said a Popsicle vendor. "And a few years ago his apple ketchup turned into red enamel house paint!"

"That was hilarious!" cried the older man. "I laughed for hours! And don't you remember his apple French toast?"

"How could I forget?" said the vendor. "My son the

wrestler tells me that it makes wonderful kneepads!"

By now everyone in the immediate area was laughing so hard they were having trouble standing up.

"Ignore them, sir," Stanley said. "They're rotten people."

John Applefeller slowly turned his head to face Stanley, his eyes glazed with a deep sadness. Through the years, Applefeller had entered a series of what he felt were highly original desserts—oatmeal-glazed, strawberry-flavored caramel apples, baked apples with peach filling, bright orange applesauce, apple ketchup, apple-flavored chocolate mousse, apple ice cream, apple Popsicles coated with apple chewing gum, apple French toast, a hollowed-out apple filled with apple yogurt, and an apple soufflé stuffed with melted chocolate and fried blueberries. But year after year, contest after contest, Applefeller's desserts had changed into something else at the last second.

Ironically, Applefeller was able to make a modest living from his failed desserts. He sold the orange applesauce that had turned into cement to a local highway crew for the construction of a new interstate freeway. His apple ketchup red enamel house paint was used to paint Appleton Elementary School. And he got an especially good price from the United States Olympic Team for his French toast kneepads.

"They may be rotten people, Stanley," Applefeller said,

"but what they said is true. I don't know how it happens, but it happens. Why can't I make a dessert that stays a dessert?"

2 · Inside the Stadium

"THIS YEAR your dessert will stay a dessert, sir," Stanley said. "You wait and see."

"I hope so, Stanley," Applefeller said. "How I hope so!"

Stanley slapped the reins and guided Morocco and their huge pancake through the contestants' gate and away from the crowd's jeers. To the left, in a booth not unlike a highway tollbooth, stood the dessert registrar, a skinny man with a large hooked nose. In front of him was a bowl of cherry mango fudge ice cream.

"Name?" the registrar asked in a high, gurgly voice.

"John Applefeller," Applefeller replied.

"Oh yes, it's you," the registrar said, suppressing a laugh. "What's your so-called dessert this year?"

"An apple pancake!" Applefeller said.

The dessert registrar stopped chewing his ice cream midchew. He looked at Applefeller blankly.

"An apple pancake? That's not a dessert, that's a breakfast!"

"Well, this pancake is a dessert!" Applefeller said. "Now if you would be kind enough to tell me where to set up, we'll be on our way."

The dessert registrar sighed. What would Applefeller think of next? He leafed through his notebook three times.

"Ah yes! Here we are. Applefeller, John—row three, position 333. That's the third row from the judges' stand on the far end of the field. Oh, and good luck to you and your apple pancake!"

The registrar was barely able to get the word *apple* out of his mouth before he started to laugh. He turned to his assistant and said, "Hey, Mac! Pass the word! Applefeller's entering an apple pancake!"

"Pay no attention to him, sir," Stanley whispered to his boss. "He's jealous of what an imaginative dessert mind you have."

Applefeller and Stanley traveled down a small slope, through a narrow tunnel, and out the entrance to the field.

Before them, hundreds of dessert chefs were lined up in three parallel lines, frantically setting up their dessert tables and making last minute preparations. Chefs barked orders at their assistants, who then scurried about getting more hot fudge sauce, more cinnamon, or more whipped cream. Midway up the field, to the right of the contestants' entrance, stood the judges' stand, a wooden platform raised four or five feet off the ground. Surrounding the great dessert grounds were rows and rows of high bleachers filled with thousands of dessert lovers. Many fans had made large signs to cheer their favorite cooks on to victory.

SYLVESTER SWEET CAN'T BE BEAT!

I AM LOCO FOR REGINALD COCO!

MICHEL DESERTS EST MAGNIFIQUE!

Throughout all of the bleachers there was only one sign cheering on John Applefeller. It was written on an old white sheet in crooked red lettering. It read:

APPLEFELLER HAS HEART!

Next to the sign stood a scruffy old man with a gray beard and old brown clothes. Next to him was a large garbage bag.

"Win! Win! Win! Johnny Applefeller—if ya catch my meanings!" the old man shouted to Applefeller in a loud voice.

"Who's that?" Applefeller asked Stanley.

"That's Josiah Benson, The Worldwide Dessert Contest janitor, sir," Stanley said.

"Why is he rooting for me?" Applefeller asked.

"I don't know, sir," Stanley replied.

"Well, as my Aunt Harriet used to say: *Never turn down support even if you don't know why they are supporting you.*"

"Good thinking, sir," Stanley said.

Applefeller turned and waved back to Josiah Benson, "Thank you very much!"

Stanley hit the reins, and Morocco moved down one of the rows toward their place on the far end of the field. As the little cart went by, more people shouted out:

"Oh, there's John Applefeller again!"

"Why doesn't he give up?"

"What's that dessert he has?"

"Don't know. But whatever it is now, it's going to be something else later!"

Applefeller stared straight ahead, determined not to let the shouts bother him.

"After I've won the Silver Spoon," he said to Stanley, "people will know what this dessert is."

"That's the spirit, sir," Stanley replied, bringing the cart to a halt by row three, position 333.

Applefeller unfolded a large table. Then he and Stanley stood on opposite sides of the cart and grabbed the pancake by its edges.

"When we lift the pancake onto the table, Stanley," Applefeller said, "do what I do. If this pancake tears in any way the spongeosity will be entirely ruined!"

"Yes sir," Stanley replied.

Slowly, after a count of three, they lifted the great dessert. But the pancake proved to be quite heavy and Applefeller stumbled backward, dropping onto his knees. The pancake's middle sagged, nearly touching the ground.

"Careful, sir!" Stanley cried.

The crowd began to laugh.

"Don't ruin the dessert!" one man cried. "Then we won't get to watch it change!"

Somehow Applefeller managed to ignore the onlookers and get back to his feet. With a mighty lunge, he and Stanley dropped the pancake onto their table.

"Whew!" Applefeller said, wiping his brow with a handkerchief. "We did it!"

"Yes sir," Stanley said.

Stanley unhitched Morocco, pushed the cart away to a corner of the stadium, and rejoined Applefeller.

"Now," Applefeller said as he removed the giant piece of wax paper that covered the dessert, "we must smooth out some of these tiny lumps. The flatter the pancake, the better the pancake!"

"Good thinking, sir," Stanley said.

Applefeller and Stanley got to work patting the pancake with their palms and soon the crowd's attention turned to other arrivals.

Checking in with the registrar after a long journey from eastern India were Reginald Coco and his assistant, Razine. Reginald Coco was tall, with a thin mustache. Razine was short, with muttonchop sideburns. Each man wore a flowing white gown and a clean white chef's cap on his head. Reginald and Razine's dessert was a chocolate covered strawberry upside-down cake à la mode with pecan ice cream. As Reginald walked onto the dessert grounds, a television reporter stopped him for a quick interview.

"Reginald, give it to me and give it to me straight. Many people here think you can win this year. Do you think you can win? Do you think you can't win? If you do win, will it be by a lot? If you don't win will it be by a little? What will you do if you lose? What will you lose if you don't win? What will you win if you win? Give it to me and give it to me straight."

Reginald listened patiently throughout the reporter's long question. Razine stood to his side holding a large ice cream scoop in his hand.

"Dear sir," Reginald began, "I come to this harmonious dessert gathering certain that the victory shall be mine. For my dessert redefines dessert as we have come to perceive it in a holistic sense."

"Very interesting," the reporter began. "So I guess what you're saying is that your dessert tastes good."

"Precisely!" Reginald agreed. "For my inner spirit is in tune with my outer spirit, and my right spirit is in tune with my left spirit! And as you know this makes for a fine dessert!" With those words, Reginald and Razine went off to set up their table.

Back by Stanley and Applefeller, Princess Irma A. Frostina, a chef from a small fishing village in southern Germany, was setting up her famous double-chocolate whipped-cinnamon delight. (Unfortunately, Princess Frostina's dessert was famous for being terrible.) Frostina was wearing a purple gown and yellow beads. She was followed about by her assistant, who fanned her with a gold fan. Just as Applefeller was looking her way, the reporter came over to Frostina.

"I'm gonna say it right out and say it straight, Irma. Your desserts stink. Everyone knows, so there's no use denying it. Why do you keep reentering the contest? Why? What's wrong with you?"

Frostina glared at the reporter and spoke.

"This year I vin the Silver Spoon! I vin, vin, vin!"

"But every other year you lose, lose, lose!" the reporter snapped. "And what is more, you have gotten so upset that you've had to be carried off the dessert field, screaming, the past six years. Why do you keep returning? Do you like torturing yourself? Is that it? Give it to me and give it to me straight!"

Frostina leaned forward and cried:

"Silly man—you listen to Princess Irma! *This year I vill vin the Silver Spoon! Vin! Vin! Vin!*"

Frostina yelled the last *vin* directly into the reporter's

face. He took a step backward, and before he knew it Frostina's assistant swatted him across the cheek with the large gold fan.

About twenty yards away, Michel Deserts, the famous dessert chef from France, was talking to another reporter about his baked crepes with coffee ice cream and hot fudge sauce. Deserts had gray hair and a finely trimmed goatee. On his head was a brown beret. He swung a cane as he talked.

"Yes, yes, yes! *Mais oui!* My dessert this year is *très elegante!*" Deserts announced. "This year my crepe is extra sweet. I bake her for two months in my special crepe-baking oven! My coffee ice cream—she is so, so fine! I use only the freshest cream from the healthiest cows from the best farms in all of France! And of course—my hot fudge! The precise mixture of cocoa beans and sugar. What a combination! *C'est merveilleux!*"

"Well, things haven't changed much around here," Applefeller noted. "Princess Frostina and Michel Deserts are as obnoxious as ever."

"They certainly are, sir," Stanley agreed.

"Look over there!" someone nearby shouted.

Suddenly people were yelling from all around the dessert grounds:

"Where?"

"There!"

"Look on the judging platform!"

"The four judges!"

3 · The Judges

THE FOUR judges had come out of their tent and now stood calmly on the judges' stand. Each was an expert taster who had made his reputation by specializing in a different aspect of dessert.

Judge Brewster McLaughlin, an enormously fat man, had invented over one hundred strains of sugar, including red sugar, sock sugar, canary sugar, and typewriter sugar.

Hamilton Crusthardy was an expert cake taster. He was a short man with a gigantic mouth. From years of mouth exercises, Crusthardy had so greatly developed his jaw muscles that he could calculate the precise time a cake had been baked to a tenth of a second.

George Saucery was a thin, serious man who specialized in ice cream. He was well known for articles in his magazine *Dessert Week*. Two of his most famous pieces were: "A Million and One Ways to Lick the Bowl," and "Ice Cream Is Best Stored at Temperatures Below Freezing."

Judge Nathaniel Barkle, the head judge, was blessed with an infallible memory and known across the world as a veritable dessert encyclopedia. One person Judge

Barkle could never forget was John Applefeller, for Applefeller's changing desserts had caused Barkle great distress throughout the years. Only a year earlier, Applefeller's apple soufflé—the one that had turned into a giant balloon—had deflated and whooshed Barkle around the dessert grounds and into a vat of chocolate sauce. Four years earlier, Applefeller's apple ketchup house paint had spilled all over him. Eight years earlier, Barkle had had to have his jaws pried opened with a monkey wrench when Applefeller's orange applesauce turned into cement in his mouth.

But the humiliation caused by these desserts was nothing compared to the discomfort caused by Applefeller's first changing dessert—for, stuck to Barkle's left cheek-

18

bone, plain as daylight, impossible for anyone to miss, was a large brown caramel apple, its white Popsicle stick pointing toward the sky.

It was true. Tragically true.

The first year Applefeller entered the contest, his dessert was oatmeal-glazed, strawberry-flavored caramel apples. But the caramel on the apples turned into the most powerful glue ever. And when one of the apples accidentally brushed against Judge Barkle's face, it stuck there. No doctor or glue specialist could remove the apple from its position. As a result, Barkle had lived the last ten years of his life with a brown caramel apple the size of a softball attached to his face.

Now, as Barkle waited for the contest to begin, one of the less polite members of the crowd stared at the large brown apple and yelled out:

"Hey, Barkle! How does it feel to look like a hatrack?"

Through the years Barkle had come to ignore such comments. But he had not forgiven John Applefeller—hardly! As time moved on, Barkle's only consolation had been in seeing Applefeller finish last in contest after contest.

"Ah, there's John Applefeller over there now," Barkle muttered to himself as he noticed Applefeller and Stanley patting their pancake. "I don't know why in all cookies we let him reenter the contest. His desserts are dangerous—as catastrophic as curdled whipped cream on a carrot cake!"

Through the crowd Applefeller saw Barkle looking at him.

"Look, Stanley," Applefeller said, "Judge Barkle is admiring my apple pancake!"

"I'm sure that's what he's doing, sir."

Just then there was a rumbling by the dessert registrar's office. It was the *boom, boom, boom* of something large hitting the earth.

Judge Barkle stood in front of a microphone on the judges' stand.

"Ladies and gentlemen. May I introduce the winner of the Silver Spoon for the last ten years in a row with his brilliant double-chocolate-fudge-raspberry-coconut-lime swirl—Sylvester S. Sweet!"

4 · The Champion

ALL EYES in the dessert grounds turned toward the registrar's office.

"There's Sylvester Sweet!"

"What's that gray thing he's on top of?"

"That's his elephant!"

"He rides an elephant?"

"Of course he does! I thought everyone knew that!"

Just then Sylvester Sweet, winner of ten consecutive Silver Spoons, came lumbering out of the entrance tunnel on his elephant, Tuba. Sitting behind Sweet was his assistant, Dentina, a beautiful blond woman in a bright red dress. As they rode, Sweet smiled broadly beneath his mustache, showing teeth so white it seemed that they'd been brushed for three weeks straight.

After a short trot around the dessert grounds, Sweet bid his elephant to stop.

"Tuba!" he cried. "Cease to move!"

Tuba came to a smooth halt next to the judges' stand.

Dentina lowered a ladder, and Sweet gingerly walked down it. He took his place next to Nathaniel Barkle.

It was clear that Sweet had spent hours, possibly days, dressing for the contest. He had on a purple embroidered tuxedo with pink lapels and a red ruffled shirt. His cummerbund was bright silver. His shoes were black and well shined. On each of his fingers he wore a glittering ring. On top of his head, he wore a yellow turban.

And if you looked very, very closely, you could see that parts of Sweet's clothing were made of dessert! His buttons were different kinds of nuts—walnuts, almonds, pecans, and pistachios. The star in the middle of his yellow turban was a large, doughy chocolate chip cookie. The gold stripes down the sides of his purple pants were made out of an extra-savory doughnut glaze.

The crowd quieted down to hear Nathaniel Barkle introduce Sweet. Barkle spoke slowly, moving carefully so that the caramel apple never hit the microphone.

"Welcome, Mr. Sweet!" Barkle began. "As head judge it is my honor to greet you as the winner of this contest for the past ten years running. If you win again, you will be awarded your eleventh Silver Spoon!"

Barkle then reached into his inner coat pocket and took out something bright and shiny and about eight inches long. He held it above his head.

It was the Silver Spoon.

The crowd cheered as the spoon glinted in the bright

sunlight. The dessert contestants gazed at the prize with intense longing. A television camera focused on it so that everyone in the world, not only those lucky enough to be near the judges' stand, could behold its beauty. On the handle was sculpted a portrait of Zeus, the Greek god, happily eating a bowl of mint-chip ice cream. Halfway between the handle and the bowl was a delicate etching of Thomas Jefferson, our great third president, eating a slice of pumpkin pie with one hand and writing the Declaration of Independence with the other. And on the bowl were carved a smiling boy and girl eating a gigantic hot fudge sundae.

As Barkle lowered the spoon, Sweet adjusted his tuxedo and stepped in front of the microphone.

"I am sure that my great double-chocolate-fudge-raspberry-coconut-lime swirl will once again win first prize!"

Applefeller and Stanley exchanged knowing glances.

"Certainly is a modest fellow, isn't he?" Applefeller said.

"He certainly is, sir."

Morocco neighed and stomped her foot in disgust. The crowd stirred and quieted again.

"I am the crème de la crème de la crème de la crème of dessert makers!" Sweet boasted, gesturing broadly with his beringed hands. "Let's face it, shall we? No one can make a dessert as well as I! No one has *ever* been able to make a dessert as well as I! I am Sylvester S. Sweet! The King of Dessert! The Lord of 'Lick the Bowl!' The Mayor of 'Mmm Mmm Good!' The Squire of 'Seconds, Please!' *The Greatest Dessert Chef Ever!*"

Sweet finished with a giant sweep of his arms and a huge self-loving grin plastered on his face.

"Bake it like it is!" Dentina yelled.

Tuba, who was standing to the side of the judges' stand, raised his trunk high in the air and let out a shrill blast. Sweet paused to comb his hair, using the diamond ring on his left pinky finger as a mirror. He took a breath and continued.

"Yes! I am the Emperor of Excellence . . ."

Just then an old man with a grizzly beard spoke out.

It was Josiah Benson, the contest's janitor, the same man who earlier had held up the sign that read: "Applefeller Has Heart!" His voice was loud and raspy, as if he'd just swallowed a handful of gravel.

"Listen," Benson began, "I've been sweepin' up at these dessert contests for ten years. And *I* say that Sylvester Sweet isn't the best dessert chef there ever was! Not no way! Not anyhow! If ya catch my meanings!"

The crowd gasped.

"Shut up, you withered man," Sweet snapped.

Sweet motioned to Tuba, who lurched menacingly toward Benson.

"You shut up yerself!" Benson cried. "I'll speak my piece, if ya know where my meanings are! And call off that overgrown cow of yours!"

Sweet signaled Tuba to stop.

"OK, Mr. Josiah Benson—'speak yer piece,' as you so eloquently put it. Who is the greatest dessert chef of all time?"

Three television microphones were thrust in front of Benson's face.

"Captain B. Rollie Ragoon!"

Sweet's face turned white.

Benson continued: "That's right! Captain B. Rollie Ragoon! He could outbake you with both of his eyes closed, if my meanings are clear to ya! The Ragoon makes magical apple pies!"

Voices echoed through the crowd:

"Magic apple pies?"

"What do they do? Card tricks?"

"Sounds ridiculous!"

Josiah Benson waved his trash bag above his head.

"I told ya that he makes magic apple pies, and I told ya the truth! And Sylvester Sweet knows it!"

The crowd leaned forward to hear what Sweet's response would be. He was still pale. He looked as if he knew very well who this Captain B. Rollie Ragoon was. He looked as if the name made him nervous.

"Now, now," Sweet stammered, "Captain B. Rollie Ragoon may be a pretty fair chef, but his apple pies aren't nearly as good as my double-chocolate-fudge-raspberry-coconut-lime swirl! In fact," Sweet continued, regaining some of his confidence, "this Ragoon man lives far, far away. And the reason that he moved is because his desserts didn't measure up to mine. He knew he was outclassed! Out-desserted! So he dessert-deserted! He left town!"

Once again people in the crowd yelled out.

"Really!"

"But where does he live?"

"How come we've never heard of him before?"

"*Quiet!*" Sweet yelled into the microphone. The sound of his voice echoed throughout the dessert grounds long after everyone had stopped speaking.

Sweet smiled broadly.

"Just remember that this Ragoon character's level of dessertmanship is very low! What is a mere apple pie? A boring nothing! Why even an apple pie that could tap dance wouldn't stand a chance in this contest against me! I am Sylvester S. Sweet—the King of Dessert! The Captain of Consumption! The Duke of Decidedly Delicious! The Lord of 'Let me have More!' *The Undisputed Greatest Dessert Maker in the World!*"

Sweet paused for breath and out of the corner of his eye glared at Josiah Benson. Benson stared back but kept quiet. He had "spoken his piece" and knew that anyone who had cared to listen had "caught his meanings."

Back on the other side of the dessert grounds, Applefeller turned to Stanley.

"What an odd little man that Josiah Benson is. Why is he the one person here who is rooting for us?"

Before Stanley could answer, Nathaniel Barkle continued with the opening ceremonies.

"We will now have the president of Appleton Elementary School's second grade scoop out the ceremonial first dish of ice cream and say a few words about her love of dessert," Judge Barkle announced.

A blond girl walked onto the platform amid a small round of applause. Judge Barkle handed her a serving spoon, and Sweet held out a box of vanilla ice cream and a bowl. The girl took the microphone and read a short prepared speech.

"What Dessert Means to Me," the girl began.

The crowd politely quieted down.

"Dessert means getting sticky. At school, dessert means it's lunch hour and recess is the next period and I'm going outside to play freeze tag with my friends. At dinnertime, dessert means supper is over, and I don't have to taste asparagus for a whole other day! Finally, and in conclusion, dessert means freedom."

The crowd cheered.

"Well put," Judge Barkle said.

"I couldn't have said it better," Sweet agreed.

The girl took the ice cream scoop firmly in her hand, scooped out a ball of vanilla ice cream and dropped it into the bowl. Contestants and spectators alike stood and cheered. The girl grinned and licked her fingers. Sweet kissed the girl on the cheek.

"Let The Worldwide Dessert Contest begin!" Barkle shouted into the microphone.

Sweet left the platform to set up his table, and the judges began their rounds.

5 · Sweet and Stanley

THE COMPETITION continued late into the afternoon. Dessert after dessert was tasted. Contestant after contestant was eliminated. Moans, cries, and wails echoed up and down the dessert grounds from distraught dessert contestants—men and women who would have to nurse their damaged prides, dreaming of the coveted Silver Spoon, for another long year.

Because of Applefeller and Stanley's placement in row three, position 333, they were to be the last contestants judged. Right next to them was Sylvester S. Sweet.

Sweet was busy putting the finishing touches on his double-chocolate-fudge-raspberry-coconut-lime swirl, admiring it with an artist's keen eye. Dentina stood behind him, ready to obey his every dessert command. Behind her was a supply table labeled "Sweet's Sweets." On this table were fresh cream, nuts, hot fudge, icing, sugar, lemons, frosting, limes, raspberries, coconuts, chocolate sprinkles, rainbow sprinkles, custard, and chocolate—any sweet that he could possibly ask for at the last minute. Sweet rolled up the sleeves of his purple tuxedo.

"Sprinkles!" he barked.

Dentina jumped and handed him a jar of chocolate sprinkles. Sweet gingerly dashed a half a dozen or so onto his dessert.

"Walnuts!" he growled.

Dentina searched behind her on the table. She turned back at Sweet with a concerned look in her eyes.

"Walnuts!" Sweet commanded. "When I ask for walnuts I want walnuts immediately!"

Dentina stared at her feet in shame.

"There are no walnuts. I don't see any on the table," she said.

"You mean that you forgot to bring along extra walnuts?" Sweet questioned.

Dentina nodded, a pitiful, embarrassed expression on her face.

"No matter," Sweet said. With those words he looked down at his vest and fingered several of the buttons.

"Ah, here we are!" he said in triumph. He plucked one of the walnut buttons off his vest and placed it strategically by the side of a particularly juicy raspberry.

Nearby, Applefeller and Stanley were busy flattening the last tiny lump that marred their otherwise smooth pancake.

"Almost, Stanley," Applefeller said as they delicately kneaded the lump with their fingers. "Easy now. A little more. Gently . . . there we are! Finished!"

Applefeller took a step backward and admired the dessert.

"It's perfect," he exclaimed. "As smooth as silk!"

"It's the most beautiful pancake I've ever seen, sir," Stanley replied.

Just then, Sweet looked up from his dessert and saw Applefeller and Stanley. He grinned.

"Hey, Applefeller," Sweet yelled, "it's about time you finished flattening that so-called dessert! But that pancake won't be very flat after it's turned into a giant balloon! Oh sorry, I forgot. That's what happened to your apple soufflé last year!"

"Pay no attention to him, sir," Stanley said.

Applefeller tried to concentrate on his pancake. But Sweet persisted.

"Maybe it'll turn into a car so you can get rid of that shriveled horse!"

Morocco snorted. Applefeller spun around.

"Now see here!" he yelled. "You leave Morocco alone. I'd take Morocco over a car any day! And furthermore, this pancake isn't going to turn into a balloon or anything else. This is one pancake that is going to stay a pancake!"

Sweet doubled over in laughter.

"Face it, Applefeller," he mocked, "you are a nobody! A no one! A has-been! A never-was! A not-anything! A never-will-be-something! Get it through your thick head! You *cannot* make a dessert! But *I*, Sylvester Sweet, am the Earl of Exceptionally Flavorful! The Practitioner of Pastry! The Guru of 'Goodness, That's Good!' "

Sweet raised his hands above his head and clasped them together in triumph.

Applefeller tried to speak, but no words came out. He gazed blankly at Sweet and then blankly down at his shoes. Stanley, however, could not stand idly by and watch his boss be insulted. He cleaned his glasses with conviction, marched up to Sweet, and looked him squarely in the eye.

"What do you want?" Sweet sneered.

31

All eyes in the immediate area were on the two—Sweet, dessert genius, and Stanley, ten-year-old boy.

Stanley drew a deep breath. "At least," he said, "Mr. Applefeller has the courage to try new things! *He* doesn't enter the *same exact dessert every year*!"

Outwardly, Sweet looked as if Stanley's words didn't bother him at all. His thick, goopy smile remained pasted on his face at its usual angle. But Stanley noticed that the flicker in his eyes dulled for an instant.

Stanley had spoken the truth. For years Sweet had felt growing pressure to enter a new dessert. True, he had won ten years running with his double-chocolate-fudge-raspberry-coconut-lime swirl, but shouldn't he be able to win each year with a different dessert?

There was a moment of tense silence as Sweet and Stanley stood toe to toe, eye to eye.

Before Sweet could answer, Tuba leaned over a large trough of water that was standing to his side, sucked it into his trunk, and with a loud honk spurted it all over Stanley.

Sweet laughed again.

"Ha ha!" he yelled. "Good boy Tuba! Good boy! You are the Earl of Elephants!"

Stanley was dripping wet. Applefeller pulled off his apron and gave it to Stanley to dry himself. Sweet wiped his hair where he'd felt a drop of water hit him and started to walk back to his dessert table. But before he took more than three steps, someone in the crowd yelled:

"So answer the kid's question! Why do you enter the *same exact dessert every year?!*"

The words seemed to bite into Sweet. He stopped mid-step and turned to face the spectator.

"To answer your rude question," Sweet said with a bit too much confidence, "I enter the same dessert every year for a simple reason."

"Yeah? Let's hear it!" yelled another from the crowd.

Sweet forced a smile.

"As you have probably realized," he said, "my dessert-tasting taste buds are developed far beyond anyone else's. And though my double-chocolate-fudge-raspberry-coconut-lime swirl may taste absolutely perfect to you, it has not, as of yet, lived up to my personal dessert standards. When I feel that my dessert has reached the state of dessert perfection, of which only *I* can be truly aware, then I, Sylvester S. Sweet, the King of Dessert, will enter a new dessert in this contest!"

"Sure ya will!" shouted someone else from the crowd.

"I think Sweet *can't* make any other dessert!" yelled another.

Sweet grew red.

"Silence!" he screamed. "I, Sylvester S. Sweet, could win with any dessert I want. Just wait until next year!"

Sweet turned on his heel and stalked back to his dessert table.

Applefeller and Stanley grinned. Sweet had committed himself. Next year he would have to enter a new dessert.

No more double-chocolate-fudge-raspberry-coconut-lime swirl.

Applefeller and Stanley turned back to their apple pancake. But before they had taken two steps, Stanley tugged at Applefeller's coattails.

"Look sir!" he said, pointing. "The judges!"

Down the aisle came Judges Barkle, McLaughlin, Crusthardy, and Saucery. It was late afternoon. The only two contestants left to be judged were Sweet and Applefeller.

6 · Sweet Is Judged

AT THIS point in the long day, Michel Deserts, the chef from Paris, was in first place. The judges had agreed that his baked crepe with hot fudge sauce and coffee ice cream was excellent. George Saucery was so impressed with the creaminess of the ice cream that he vowed to travel to France after the contest to interview Deserts' cow.

As usual, Princess Irma Frostina did very badly. She was in 910th place.

"Zes is horrible!" Frostina wailed. "I come all the vay from Germany for vhat? To be humiliated! I vant to vin the Silver Spoon! I vant the Silver Spoon!"

And it had been an especially disappointing day for

the two Indian chefs, Reginald Coco and Razine. Their dessert hopes were smashed when Hamilton Crusthardy found a single rotten pecan in their ice cream.

The four dessert experts were understandably weary after the long day.

"Whew!" Brewster McLaughlin said, patting his very large stomach, "I don't know if I have room for another dessert!"

"You'll find it, I'm sure," quipped George Saucery. "I, however, am not sure if my intellectual faculties are up to accurately evaluating any more ice cream."

"And I'm not quite certain if my powerful mouth muscles can deduce the exact baking time of yet another cake," said Hamilton Crusthardy as he rubbed his strong yet tired jaw.

"Come, come!" Barkle said. "If I can do it, so can you. And Sylvester Sweet is next! Let's get to it!"

Barkle scratched his caramel apple and approached Sweet's dessert table. In front of him was a beautifully arranged dessert. Ten delicately cut raspberries and ten carefully sliced limes were arranged in a circle around the outside of a shining gold dish. In the middle of this elegantly ordered array of fruit was a piece of coconut cake with coconut icing—milk white and moist. On top of the cake was a heaping spoonful of chocolate ice cream. A double helping of hot fudge sauce flowed like a river in and out of the nooks and crannies between the cake, ice cream, raspberries, and limes. Finally, (the touch that gave the dessert its completeness, like all great works of art) a dollop of whipped cream was placed on top.

Extra TV cameras were called on to view this dessert from every possible angle. One cameraman lowered himself by ropes from a helicopter to capture an overhead shot.

"Well, Mr. Sweet," Barkle began, "what dessert have we this year?"

"My double-chocolate-fudge-raspberry-coconut-lime swirl, sir," Sweet replied with a smile that showed every one of his teeth. "This year my chocolate is even more chocolate-y. And the mixture of raspberries and limes is even more refined."

"I'll be the judge of that!" Barkle said, taking out his gold spoon for a first bite. (Not to be confused with the Silver Spoon, this was the selfsame utensil Barkle had used to judge the contest for ten years and had promised to donate to the Appleton Dessert Museum upon his retirement.)

In the background, Michel Deserts, Princess Irma Frostina, and other contestants looked on. The bleachers around Sweet and Applefeller groaned with the extra weight of dessert fans who had sneaked over to watch the contest's exciting climax.

Barkle reached down to the dessert and scooped out a small bite. He stared at Sweet with a serious expression as he put the spoon into his mouth. His Adam's apple bobbed up and down as he chewed, considered, and then chewed some more.

"Hmmm," he said, "the swirlosity of this dessert is most impressive."

"Thank you!" Sweet intoned. "I experimented with several different swirl formations and decided that this was the most swirly."

Barkle let his tongue glide back and forth over his teeth.

"And the coconut cake is neither too cocoed nor too nutted to overshadow the elegant lime-raspberry-chocolatemanship."

"I know!" Sweet agreed. "It is brilliant, isn't it?"

Barkle swallowed the rest of his mouthful and wrinkled his brow in deep thought. After a few moments he shook his head in disbelief and grinned.

"Sweet," he said, "I don't know how you do it, but you do it. You're in a class by yourself. This is delicious— truly delicious! Historically speaking, I would compare this dessert to the double-chocolate-fudge-raspberry-coconut-lime swirl that Davy Crockett ate at the Alamo!"

"That is precisely the taste I was going for," Sweet confided.

A short round of applause rippled through the crowd. Dentina and Tuba smiled proudly at their boss. Barkle stepped aside and Brewster McLaughlin strode up and staked out a large piece of ground in front of Sweet's dessert.

"I think you'll find that my sugars are blended in a most blendable fashion," Sweet informed him.

McLaughlin patted his round belly with pride. "If they are well blended," he said, "I'm certainly the man to tell it. If I do say so myself, I know my sugar!"

With those words McLaughlin carved a large portion and put it in his mouth. He chewed with great gusto and came to a quick conclusion.

"Excellent!" he said. "The confection quality of this dessert is highly blendable! And I taste eighteen different strains of sugar, including shoelace sugar, which I invented myself!"

"Yes!" Sweet smiled. "Actually there are nineteen strains of sugar, but who's counting?"

McLaughlin's eyes opened and closed.

"Nineteen strains?" he said.

"Of course," Sweet replied. "No doubt you overlooked floor sugar, the taste of which was delicately covered by rug sugar."

Brewster McLaughlin moved aside, shaking his head, vowing to review his sugar encyclopedia after the contest.

It was now the turn of the cake expert, Hamilton Crusthardy. He stepped up and exchanged a nod with Sweet. Then, with a mighty, rippling flex of his jaw, he took a bite. Everyone in the dessert grounds was standing now, listening intently. But they didn't have to listen hard, because Hamilton Crusthardy's cry of dessert ecstasy could be heard all the way to the other side of town.

"Ahhhhhhhhhhhhhhhhhhhhhhhhhhh!" he screamed. "This cake was obviously baked for one hour and three minutes at four hundred degrees! And the icing on the cake is just icy enough to complement the double-fudgitude!"

"How perceptive you are!" Sweet crowed. "The icing-to-hot-fudge ratio was measured precisely on my home computer."

Sweet was all smiles now. Dentina rubbed the back of his neck and grinned. Tuba squatted confidently by his side. But everyone in the dessert grounds knew that Sweet could not afford to relax yet, for George Saucery, the most difficult judge of them all, was still to take his last licks.

As Saucery approached Sweet's table, the crowd grew so quiet you could hear ice cream melt. Even Sweet himself nervously fingered his shiniest emerald ring. Judge Barkle patted Saucery on the shoulder.

"It's all up to you," he said.

Saucery nodded and, spoon in hand, reached for Sweet's dessert. Four television cameras focused as closely as they could on Saucery's mouth as he took his bite and began to chew up and down in a careful, steady motion. He paused and scratched his chin. He rubbed his spoon over his lips. He curled his tongue and rubbed it across his teeth. Then he chewed some more. The fans were finding it hard to keep still. How much longer could it take? One minute passed. Two minutes! Three! Finally, after four minutes, Saucery spoke.

"The ice cream is superb!" he declared. "The dessert is superb! Personally, there's nothing I'd rather eat!"

The dessert grounds erupted into wild applause. Dessert fans pounded on the bleachers, cheering. Cameras clicked a picture a second and reporters shouted into their microphones. The four judges gathered around Sweet to shake his hand. He had won the Silver Spoon for the eleventh year in a row.

"Thank you! Thank you!" Sweet gushed. "I owe it all to myself and my great dessert-making genius!"

The fans in the bleachers broke into a chant: "Sylvester Sweet—Dessert King!"

Tuba lifted Sweet up by his trunk, placed him on his head, and began trotting him around the dessert grounds. Sweet spread his arms out wide.

"I am the Sultan of Silver Spoons!" he cried.

Everyone was happy, celebrating the glorious victory. Fans shook hands with policemen. Policemen slapped backs with reporters. Reporters congratulated each other, all as though they had won the prize themselves.

But a handful of defeated chefs didn't share the festive mood. Michel Deserts was very upset.

"*Zut alors!*" he moaned, throwing his cane on the ground. "I always lose to that Sweet man and his lime-raspberry swirl!"

And Princess Irma Frostina caused a small commotion by jumping in her dessert and screaming in German. But before she got too much out of control, she was dragged off the field by three policemen.

After Frostina had been carted away, Barkle spoke: "Now for the presentation of the Silver Spoon!"

Tuba laid Sweet down in front of the judges. The crowd hushed and stood on tiptoes to see. Sweet combed his hair, using the crystal ring on his right pinky as a mirror, and straightened the left lapel of his purple tuxedo.

"I, Head Judge Nathaniel Barkle do declare Sylvester S. Sweet . . ."

"*Wait!*"

Barkle stopped speaking midsentence. All eyes turned toward the voice. Who said that? How dared anyone interrupt the Silver Spoon ceremony?

It was John Applefeller.

"What do you want?" Barkle asked angrily.

"You haven't judged my apple pancake yet. It's the largest apple pancake in the world!"

There was a deep silence in the dessert grounds. The only noise was the muffled sound of people trying not to laugh. The four judges looked at each other with a decided lack of enthusiasm. Their taste buds were tasted out for the afternoon. They wanted to rest, to go home and eat dinner. On top of it all, they were sure that Applefeller's dessert would be terrible.

"Come now! Let's get on with the ceremony!" Sweet demanded. "I am the King of Dessert, and I want the Silver Spoon!"

"Fair is fair, sirs," Stanley said with conviction. "You have to judge our dessert!"

Barkle sighed.

"He's right. He's right. We have one more dessert— at least I think it's a dessert—to taste. John Applefeller's apple pancake. Come on. Let's get this over with."

7 · The Apple Pancake

THE FOUR judges walked wearily over to John Applefeller's table. All the remaining spectators and contestants strained to see, everyone secretly hoping that Applefeller's dessert would backfire for the eleventh year in a row and turn into something else. A television reporter went on the air: "Well, it looks like the real contest is over and now it's time for the comic relief!"

A crowd member cried out: "Hey, Judge Barkle. You think you look bad now? Just wait until you have an apple pancake attached to your face!"

The back of Barkle's neck turned red, for ever since

Applefeller's apple had become a permanent fixture on his cheek, he had not been able to taste any of Applefeller's desserts with steady nerves. He stepped gingerly up to the apple pancake and looked it over.

Brewster McLaughlin followed Barkle and slapped him on the back.

"Come on there, Nathaniel! What are you afraid of?"

Muffled laughter rippled through the crowd.

"Nothing at all!" Barkle said. "I shall take the first bite!"

Sylvester Sweet smiled a wry smile and started signing autographs.

Applefeller and Stanley stood on either side of the table, too excited to move.

Barkle took out his gold spoon and tried to cut into the pancake.

"A knife and fork may help," Applefeller suggested.

"Yes, quite," Barkle agreed.

Brewster McLaughlin handed Barkle the utensils. Barkle bent down over the pancake, his black robe fluttering in the cool late afternoon breeze, and cut. He lifted the fork and looked at the golden brown pancake on its end, as if he were making up his mind whether it was safe to eat. Then, just as he was about to put it into his mouth, Barkle gave Applefeller a sideways glance.

"Shouldn't there be syrup on this?"

"No sir," Applefeller responded, "the syrup and the apples are baked directly into the pancake."

"Into the pancake, you say?" Barkle retorted with a raised right eyebrow (the eye that was unaffected by the caramel apple). "Interesting, very interesting. Well, here goes nothing."

Barkle closed his eyes and grimaced like a little child being forced by his mother to eat brussels sprouts. He raised the fork to his mouth, held it there below his nose for a moment, and then, quick as a flash, before he could change his mind, he put the pancake into his mouth. With his eyes still closed he chewed as fast as he could. But after a second, he started chewing a little slower and then a little slower still. His horrible grimace became a smile.

Barkle was enjoying the pancake! Applefeller and Stanley looked at each other hopefully. The crowd sensed that something was different with Applefeller's dessert this year—it was good!

Sylvester Sweet stopped signing autographs to see what was causing such a stir.

"What do you think? How is it?" Brewster Mc-Laughlin asked as Barkle chewed on, now with a broad grin on his face.

"I have to admit it!" Barkle said. "This is a very nice dessert! It is golden brown, yet neither so golden nor so brown as to render the desired effect negligible."

"That good, eh?" George Saucery asked with an impressed upward turn of his brow.

"Yes! Yes!" Barkle smiled. "Applefeller, this is a fine dessert! Truly fine!"

"Why, thank you," Applefeller replied. "I've worked so hard . . ."

"Here, give me another bite," Barkle said. "The taste of this pancake is so subtle that I cannot yet think of what to compare it to."

"Certainly," Applefeller chimed.

Stanley cut a bigger piece for Barkle to taste.

Barkle took the piece and chewed it eagerly.

"Yes! I've got it now!" Barkle announced. "Historically speaking, I would compare the taste of this pancake to the taste of the apple pancakes eaten by Abraham Lincoln before delivering the Gettysburg Address!"

Applefeller's face was aglow. Such high praise!

"Here, have one more bite, sir," Stanley said.

"Don't mind if I do. Thank you, boy," Barkle said warmly.

The crowd murmured. Three bites! Three bites! Barkle took three bites of Applefeller's dessert! This was unheard of. One bite was standard and two bites highly unconventional. Barkle had never asked for three bites of Sylvester Sweet's double-chocolate-fudge-raspberry-coconut-lime swirl!

The color drained from Sylvester Sweet's face.

The other judges held their utensils in the air, anxious to try some too.

"There now, Barkle—fair is fair. You've had your turn. Give us a chance!" George Saucery demanded, pointing his spoon toward Barkle.

"Yes, I must evaluate the sweetness of the pancake," announced Brewster McLaughlin.

"OK, OK!! Don't rush me! You'll get your chance. It's just that this pancake is so marvelously good! So fantastically wonderful! Hey, you there, boy," Barkle said to Stanley, "could I have just *one* more tiny bite?"

"Of course, sir."

Four bites!!!

"Hurry up now!" Brewster McLaughlin demanded.

"In a second," Barkle replied.

"This is ridiculous!" Sweet muttered. "My brilliance cannot be beaten by a pancake. It's impossible!"

But it *was* possible! In fact, it was happening. Barkle put the fourth piece of apple pancake into his mouth, and as he chewed, he talked enthusiastically.

"My, *what* a dessert! It's sweet yet not cloying. Light yet just heavy enough to be substantial! Fluffy yet manageable! Delicate yet convincing! It's magnificent! A dessert masterpiece! It's a . . ."

Just then Barkle stopped short and felt the corner of his mouth.

"What's wrong?" Crusthardy asked.

"I don't know! But suddenly this pancake has become a little more difficult to chew."

"Really now?" Brewster McLaughlin said.

"Yes," Barkle responded with a worried look. "In fact, I would say that a certain rubbery texture is beginning to be highly prevalent!"

Now Applefeller and Stanley looked worried. Sylvester Sweet's wrinkled brow unwrinkled a bit. The crowd started whispering. Had something gone wrong with Applefeller's dessert again?

Barkle could barely move his jaw now. He opened his mouth to speak but couldn't. With great effort he gasped, "Help me."

Brewster McLaughlin rushed over with his own bronze tasting spoon in hand to pry open Barkle's mouth. It took all of McLaughlin's massive bulk and muscle power to wrench Barkle's mouth open far enough to remove the remains of a partially chewed piece of apple pancake.

"Thank you!" Barkle said, greatly relieved.

All eyes in the dessert grounds strained to see what was dangling there on the end of McLaughlin's bronze spoon. What was once a delicious piece of apple pancake now looked like a mangled piece of bicycle tire.

McLaughlin approached the pancake, knife and fork in hand.

"Let me see what's going on here," he said.

With a powerful sawing motion, McLaughlin tried to cut into the pancake—he couldn't!

"Seems to be rubber!" he announced.

The crowd gasped. Applefeller looked down at his shoes. His embarrassment grew when McLaughlin took out his fork and dropped it onto the pancake. Instead of just lying there it bounced smack into McLaughlin's face.

"What the sprinkles!" McLaughlin fumed.

The crowd's mood changed right along with the change in the pancake. People started laughing.

"Drop it again and move your head out of the way this time," George Saucery suggested.

McLaughlin took a step back and tossed the fork onto the pancake. It bounced thirty feet into the air.

The crowd cheered and started stamping on the bleachers. Sylvester Sweet laughed and wiped his brow in relief. Once again Applefeller had made a fool of himself.

Barkle glared at Applefeller.

"Your giant apple pancake appears to be a trampoline. I suggest that you sell it to Goode's Sporting Goods. I'm sure they would find it quite marketable!"

"It was supposed to be a dessert," Applefeller sighed.

Sweet was grinning from ear to ear and clasping his hands above his head. Now it was official. He had won the dessert contest for eleven years running. Tuba, excited, raised his trunk and blew loudly. Then he charged across the field to where Nathaniel Barkle was standing with his back turned. *Boom!* Tuba hit Barkle from behind and onto the apple pancake! *Bounce!* Up Barkle went! Up, up, up, up, up—at least ninety feet, his black robe waving wildly in the breeze.

The children were bouncing twenty at a time. Unlike Nathaniel Barkle, they loved the way it felt to fly high in the air.

"Whee! What a ride!"

"I never had so much fun with a pancake before!"

Suddenly, Brewster McLaughlin surprised everyone by announcing that he wanted a try. He pushed to the front of the line.

"Hey, mister, wait your turn!" a brave child yelled as McLaughlin moved past him.

"Quiet!" McLaughlin shouted. "I shall ride this pancake. I never got to taste it, so at the very least I should be given the opportunity to jump on it!"

The children could not refute the logic of that statement.

"Here we go!" McLaughlin yelled. He took a great leap, his fat stomach hitting square in the middle of the pancake.

Boom!

His bulk gave him great bouncing power. Up he went. One hundred and twenty feet into the air. The children shrieked with delight.

"Way to go, mister!"

"What a pancake!"

"Yippee!" McLaughlin yelled. "This pancake may not be sweet, but the bounceability factor is very, *very* high!"

Boom! Up McLaughlin sailed again. This time one hundred feet.

Applefeller sat alone, not even able to look Stanley in the eye. Suddenly, he was surrounded by newspaper reporters.

"Applefeller, give it to us and give it to us straight. Why do your desserts change? Why don't your desserts stay desserts? Why do other people's desserts stay desserts? What's wrong with you? Give it to us straight."

Before Applefeller could answer, Stanley chased the reporters away.

"Leave Mr. Applefeller be!" he yelled. Then Morocco grabbed one of the reporter's cameras in his mouth and smashed it against the ground. After some loud complaining, the rude newsmen ran off to interview someone else.

But Applefeller wasn't to be left alone yet, for when Nathaniel Barkle finally managed to get off the apple pancake and away from the crowd, he strode over to Applefeller, his clothes dishevelled, his hair mussed up, his face red with anger.

"Applefeller!" Barkle fumed. "This is the last straw! I have been hurt and humiliated by your desserts long enough! If I can possibly arrange it, you will never, *ever* enter this contest again! *Never!*"

He stalked off without waiting for a response.

The line to jump on Applefeller's pancake was now three hundred feet long and growing. Applefeller looked at it in complete misery. Stanley's soothing words and Morocco's gentle presence provided little comfort. It was true that John Applefeller had made the greatest trampoline ever. But he didn't care about that. What John Applefeller cared about were desserts—apple desserts. And now it looked like Judge Barkle might arrange it so he could never enter the contest again.

Just then a small girl with pigtails ran over to Applefeller.

"Hey, mister!" the girl said. "Thank you for the pancake. It's so bouncy!"

Applefeller looked into the girl's smiling face and not wanting to seem impolite said, "Thank you, my dear. Thank you. I'm glad you're enjoying it."

After the girl turned and ran back to get on line for another bounce, Applefeller looked sadly up at Stanley.

"It was supposed to be a dessert," he sighed. "It was supposed to be a dessert!"

8 · Applefeller Makes a Decision

"HEY, YOU THERE!" a voice called.

Through the crowd walked the one man who had rooted for Applefeller during the contest—the man who had interrupted Sylvester Sweet—Josiah Benson, The Worldwide Dessert Contest janitor. Benson carried with him the tool of his trade, a large gray trash bag.

"Hey, you there!" he repeated. "You look at me, if ya catch my meanings!"

Stanley stepped in front of his boss.

"Not now. I don't think Mr. Applefeller wants to speak to anyone just yet."

"Well, he'll change his mind when he hears what I have to say," Benson exclaimed. With that he walked up to Applefeller and stood directly in front of him. "There, there!" Benson continued. "Don't look so downcast! Don't look so gloomy! You've only begun to fight! You've only begun to cook desserts!"

"Oh, I don't know," Applefeller said. "For eleven years—*eleven years*—I've finished in last place. It's embarrassing! As my Aunt Harriet used to say: *Winning isn't everything, but if you never win then you might consider giving up.*"

"Don't say that, sir," Stanley said.

Morocco sighed heavily and looked at Applefeller, heavy tears welling up in her big brown eyes.

"So you're a quitter, eh?" Benson said with a wry smile. "I didn't think you would be a quitter! Captain B. Rollie Ragoon isn't a quitter, if my meanings are clear to ya. If he was a quitter wouldn't he have quit when folks said his magical roller-skating apple pies were a gimmick? Yes! Wouldn't he have quit when folks said his apple pies that could speak four different languages really couldn't speak four different languages? Yes! Yes! Yes, if my intent is crystal clear! Well, frankly, I'm tempted now *not* to tell you where this Captain B. Rollie Ragoon lives!"

During Josiah Benson's speech Applefeller's eyes had begun to light up.

"Captain B. Rollie Ragoon!" Applefeller said. "You mean that magical apple pie chef you mentioned during Sweet's opening speech?"

"Yes—Captain B. Rollie Ragoon!" Benson confirmed. "He's the greatest apple pie chef ever if ya know where my meanings are. You see, your problem, Applefeller, is not that you don't have talent—you have a lot of talent. Remember, Judge Barkle thought your dessert was great until it changed at the last minute. But why do they change? You don't know why! So you need a teacher. Someone to show ya how to make an original dessert that won't change."

"But I've run out of ideas," Applefeller said. "I've tried every original dessert I can think of!"

"All the more reason you should go," Benson said. "The Ragoon would inspire ya! After ten minutes in his bakery you'll have fifty new ideas!"

"Well, maybe," Applefeller replied.

"But where is this Captain Ragoon?" Stanley asked. "And not only that, *who* is he?"

"This Ragoon feller is an odd one alrighty," Benson began. "But he's a good man. And boy, can he cook! Up till about fifteen years ago he used to live not too far away from here. But as soon as he heard they were gonna start this dessert contest, he got disgusted. He knew that since he was the best chef around he'd feel compelled to enter and he wanted to cook desserts for his own pleasure, not for any prizes. So one day he made himself a decision. Off he went far away to a land where he said he'd be able to cook in peace."

"But do his pies really roller-skate?" Applefeller asked.

"Sure as shootin' they do!" Benson said.

"And they speak different languages?" Stanley inquired.

"Hoppin' catfish, yes!" Benson said.

"But is that really possible?" Applefeller questioned. "Forgive me, but that's a lot to ask a man to believe."

"Well, ya gotta believe it!" Benson said. "What I'm telling you is the truth. The *real* truth. I know that this

Ragoon can help ya. He's as talented as a herd of snortin' cowdogs!"

Applefeller looked at Benson and then at the line of people waiting to bounce on his pancake. He couldn't stand the spectacle. Maybe the Ragoon would give him some new ideas or at least show him how to make a dessert that didn't change.

"Well," Applefeller said, "maybe you're right. But do you think this Ragoon man will be willing to help me?"

"I would think so, if I recommend ya," Benson said.

"Why would you want to help us?" Stanley asked.

Benson sighed and looked around him.

"It's no life," he said, "pickin' up the soggy ice cream cartons and sticky cake boxes of messy, mean people like Sylvester Sweet. Sure, I do my job 'cause I have to make my money. But I've been wantin' to visit the Ragoon for a while, and I need some people to travel with."

"But how do you know him?" Stanley asked.

"Oh, me and the Ragoon go back a long way. And he said that if I or any of my friends ever wanted to visit it would be fine."

"But where is this place?" Applefeller asked.

Josiah Benson reached into his shirt pocket and took out a folded piece of yellow paper that was tattered at the edges. He carefully unfolded it and spread it out on Applefeller's lap.

"This here is the map the Ragoon gave me before he

went away," Benson said. "I'm the only feller alive who knows where he is."

In the corner of the map was writing in blue ink.

"This here is the Ragoon's signature," Benson said.

Both Applefeller and Stanley looked closely at the piece of paper.

Then Benson pointed his long bony finger toward a spot marked with a circle.

"This is Appleton," he said.

"Where's the Ragoon?" Applefeller asked.

"Over here," Benson answered, jabbing at a spot on the other side of the paper no bigger than a pencil point.

Applefeller and Stanley exchanged glances.

"What's in between?" Stanley asked.

"The ocean," Benson replied.

"The ocean!" Applefeller said. "So the Ragoon lives on an island?"

"Absolutely! Where did ya think he was?" Benson inquired.

"But how in the world do we get there?" Applefeller asked.

"Well," Josiah Benson said thoughtfully, "no airline or boat company knows where this place is. And none of us has the money to get a private boat or plane. So it's a problem. Got any suggestions?"

Applefeller and Stanley were quiet for a minute, thinking.

"It's a toughie," Benson said. "No question about it. But there must be some way."

After thirty more seconds of hard thought Applefeller sighed and shook his head.

"It's more than a toughie. It's impossible. We can't swim there and we certainly can't ride there on a dessert!"

At the mention of the word *dessert* Stanley's eyes lit up.

"What did you just say, sir?"

"I said we can't swim . . ."

"No sir—the dessert part."

"What dessert part?" Applefeller said.

"You said that we can't ride there on a dessert. But we can!"

"What are you sayin'?" Benson asked. "How can someone ride a dessert?"

Stanley spoke quickly.

"We can take Mr. Applefeller's apple soufflé that turned into a balloon in last year's contest, inflate it with helium, attach it to Morocco's cart, and fly to the Ragoon's island!"

"That's crazy!" Applefeller said.

"No," Stanley said. "It'll work, sir. I've seen the balloon lying in your barn. We'll ride your dessert to the Ragoon's island!"

"Well, cover me with lettuce and throw me to the

rabbits!" Benson exclaimed, pulling on his beard with short frantic tugs. "It's beautiful! As beautiful as a flock of skippin' horsetoads! Now if my memory serves me correctly, that balloon was twenty feet wide and forty feet tall. The perfect size!"

"It'll never work!" Applefeller said.

"Dancin' horsepuppies it won't!" Benson shouted. "Stanley, you're a regular genius!"

"Thank you, Mr. Benson, sir," Stanley said.

Stanley and Josiah Benson shook hands. Applefeller turned and walked a few steps in the opposite direction. He needed a minute to think. First, he had almost won the Silver Spoon with the most original dessert ever. Then a funny janitor had told them to travel to a far-off island in search of a strange man named Captain B. Rollie Ragoon. Then Stanley, usually a sensible boy, had suggested that they get there by riding an apple-soufflé balloon!

Applefeller lifted his head and looked off as far as he could into the twilight. The sun was setting, and there to his left, silhouetted against the orange-streaked sky, was his pancake. Applefeller turned to face his colossal failure. Children were still bouncing on it, and reporters were still taking its picture. Applefeller shook his head. Morocco came up and nuzzled him. Stanley and Josiah Benson stood expectantly nearby.

"Shall we go to find this Ragoon man, sir?" Stanley

asked finally. "I should be able to get permission from my parents. They love adventures as much as I do."

Applefeller took one final glance at his pancake.

"Go . . . of course we're going! We have no choice, right? I'm not a quitter, and I can't keep making changing desserts my whole life. If this Ragoon fellow can help, then so be it. I believe in desserts. And as my Aunt Harriet used to say: *If you truly believe in something, then you should act as if you truly believe in it!*"

"Well, cover me with horses and lead me to the blacksmith!" Josiah Benson exclaimed. "That's good news!"

"When do we start, sirs?" Stanley asked.

"Now, if not sooner!" Applefeller said. "We have a lot to do! We need to set up the balloon. We need supplies. Not to mention rope, wood, food, clothing, grain . . ."

"Grain?" Benson asked.

"Of course, grain," Applefeller said. "For Morocco! I could never leave her behind. And besides, if we take Morocco, we can hitch her back to the cart when we reach the Ragoon's island. The island may be big, and we'll need a quick way to get around."

"Good thinking, sir."

"Well, then, let's get to it!" Benson said.

Applefeller and his crew walked to their cart in the corner of the stadium. Stanley hitched up Morocco and they climbed aboard. As Applefeller slapped the reins, he looked overhead. . . . The first stars were beginning to shine. His gaze fixed on The Big Dipper. Applefeller imagined that the six stars of the constellation made up the outlines of the Silver Spoon. Then he imagined the Silver Spoon hanging up in his living room over his fireplace.

"Next year's going to be different!" he said with conviction. "No more changing desserts!"

"That's the spirit, sir!"

"Now you're talkin'! Now you're talkin'!" Benson yelled.

"Giddyap, Morocco!" Applefeller exclaimed.

Morocco broke into a trot, and the cart sped homeward through the cool, clear night.

PART
TWO

9 · The Apple Balloon

ALTHOUGH the adventurous trio wanted to leave immediately, Stanley's mother had different ideas.

"Not until you finish fifth grade," she stated. "Then you and that nice Mr. Applefeller can take his lovely apple balloon anywhere you'd like. Now eat your ice cream."

Stanley knew his mother well enough to know it was no use arguing. The only thing to do was to tell Applefeller and Josiah Benson to go ahead without him.

"Jumpin' cowdogs, no!" Josiah Benson cried. "We're a team—where we go, you go!"

"Absolutely!" Applefeller agreed. "We'll delay the trip until June."

"And it won't make a bit of difference anyhow," Josiah Benson exclaimed. "If we leave early enough in June, we'll still have plenty of time to find the Ragoon, get his help, and be back for the contest in mid-July!"

So the three put their plans on hold for ten months and fell into their separate routines. Josiah Benson picked up trash, Applefeller made a new supply of French toast kneepads for the United States Olympic team, and Stanley went to school.

The year passed quickly enough.

One morning in late May, Applefeller rolled the cart out of the barn to the middle of his front yard. There he nailed four wooden planks to its four edges, making a five-foot-high railing. Then he brought on a tent, three sleeping bags, a small wood stove, food, and hay for Morocco.

"This here is the first horse's cart that's also convertible for air travel," Benson declared, once he'd seen Applefeller's handiwork. "Now I'll get to work attachin' the balloon."

Benson dragged Applefeller's deflated soufflé out of storage and patched the rip. Then he tied it to the cart and filled it with helium (making sure to tie the cart to the ground first, so it wouldn't go flying away). Finally, Benson rigged up the steering by attaching two ropes to either side of the balloon. Pulling on either rope would cause the balloon to lean in that direction and turn that way. Benson then put a full tank of helium directly under a hole in the bottom of the balloon. To go higher, all they had to do was turn the helium on.

When he was finished, Benson grinned. If he said so himself, he had done a fine job. All for a good cause too—dessert.

"It's a flying house!" Applefeller said the next morning as he admired the balloon cart floating six inches off the ground.

"Yessiree!" Benson agreed. "And today's the day Stanley finishes up at school. We can leave tomorrow!"

Stanley arrived right on time the next morning. He was a year older and two inches taller. He had a thicker pair of glasses perched on his nose. In fifth grade he had learned that Thomas Jefferson more than doubled the size of America with the Louisiana Purchase, that a negative number times a positive number equals a negative number, and that *"Regardez! J'ai une voiture!"* means "Look! I have a car!" in French. But none of these important facts had dampened his enthusiasm for dessert and for the trip to see the Ragoon.

"What a balloon, sirs!" Stanley exclaimed.

"No dessert chef has ever had a more elegant mode of transportation," Applefeller agreed.

"Absolutely!" Benson replied. "Now let's go! No time to dillydally—none at all. We have a few states to fly over today."

Stanley brought Morocco from the barn, and after some coaxing she jumped up onto the cart, which swayed back and forth roughly under the force of her leap. Josiah Benson and Stanley reached for the cart's sides to steady it.

"Now are ya sure we've got everything?" Benson asked.

"Oh yes," Applefeller said, climbing aboard, "we're all set."

"Then let's go!" Benson cried.

He and Stanley jumped onto the cart. They each grabbed one of the two ropes tying it to the ground. When these were cut, they would be off.

"Ready?" Benson yelled.

"Ready!" Stanley said.

Applefeller took one last look around. "Ready!" he confirmed.

Benson and Stanley cut the ropes and Applefeller turned on the helium control for extra lift-off power. Slowly and evenly, the cart began to rise.

"Steady now, Johnny!" Benson said. "Steady!"

Applefeller fiddled with the steering and straightened out the great balloon. He saw his house and barn become smaller and smaller. Within seconds the beautiful country landscape spread below them in every direction—tall pine trees, grassy meadows, green mountains. Applefeller grinned.

"This is great!" he yelled.

"Isn't it, sir?" Stanley said as he leaned his head over the railing.

"Bring us over to the left there, Johnny," Benson exclaimed. "Left! Left!"

Applefeller gently tugged the left rope and let more helium up into the balloon. They rose quickly—two men, one boy, their horse, their cart, and their red apple-soufflé balloon—in search of Captain B. Rollie Ragoon and ideas for an original but nonchanging dessert.

10 · Iambia
(Pronounced I-*am*-bee-uh)

SOON THE great balloon was flying over farms and pastures on the outskirts of Appleton, moving at the speed of a fast train. The scenery rushed by.

"Yippee!" Benson shouted as the wind blew back his gray hair and beard. "This sure beats pickin' up trash!"

"I should say so, sir!" Stanley agreed. "Not nearly as messy either!"

"As my Aunt Harriet used to say: *Nine out of ten people would greatly prefer riding in a balloon to picking up garbage!*"

"Absolutely, sir!"

"Sure as a firefly in August, if my intentions have their clarity!"

"Positively, sir!"

"Look down there!"

"Where?"

"There!" Applefeller said, pointing toward some farmers who had stopped weeding their new corn to look up at the great balloon in astonishment. "Boy, do they ever wish they were up here with us! Eat your hearts out!" he yelled down.

"What's that?" people cried.

"Looks like a flying barn!" others said.

"But horses can't fly!"

"The horse isn't flying, stupid, the barn is!"

Applefeller, Stanley, and Josiah Benson got a good many laughs staring down at the surprised faces. All three took turns maneuvering the balloon; all three mastered the art of pulling the directional ropes and adding more helium at the same time. The first hours of the trip were a decided success. Once a large bird flew into the cart and gave Morocco a scare, but aside from that she seemed to enjoy the ride as much as her three companions. She put her head out over the edge and let the wind blow back her mane. And the wind was strong.

"I would conjecture we've passed three states already!" Benson said that afternoon.

"No!"

"Yessiree, if ya catch my longitudes!"

"This is one fast balloon, sir!" Stanley said.

"It was supposed to be a dessert, but I accept the compliment."

Josiah Benson referred to the map often and kept them on a steady course.

"Turn her right there, Johnny. Easy now," he would cry. "Now left, if my words have their meanings."

On they flew over wide lakes, green parks, red barns, and busy cities, making their way westward.

"Let's stop until the morning," Josiah Benson said as evening drew on. "We don't want to bump into any trees!"

Applefeller navigated the balloon into a meadow. As the first stars began to shine, Stanley lit a small fire in the stove and cooked their supper. Before bed they sat in front of the tent by the warm glow of the stove and told stories—stories of great desserts and great dessert chefs of bygone days.

At dawn they woke from happy dessert dreams and got to work. Morning was pleasant traveling time. The air was cool and the sky and clouds were streaked with orange.

Two days passed quickly. During the third morning they came to the Pacific Ocean.

"We should be there any time now, if ya hear my words," Josiah Benson said as he consulted the map.

That afternoon a tiny speck of land appeared in the midst of the blue sea.

"Jumping hummingbirds!" Benson exclaimed.

"What!"

"What?"

"*Look!*"

He pointed at a small dot to the west.

"I think that's it!"

"Really?"

"If ya got my directions, it is!"

"Pump more helium, Stanley!"

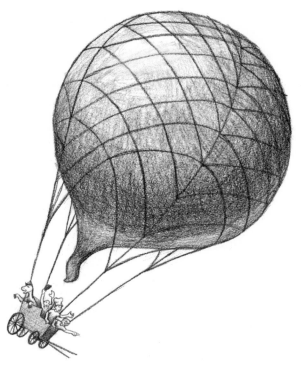

The balloon whizzed through the air, and soon they all saw the clear definition of a very tiny island. It was tropical and lush with green vegetation. Beneath them loomed a densely wooded forest.

"Where are the people?" Applefeller asked. "Are you sure this is the right place?"

"Sure as a horsefly in a bucket, if ya hear my latitudes!"

Applefeller nodded, encouraged by Josiah Benson's confidence, and kept the balloon on a steady course above the ever-rising thicket of trees, until suddenly the three travelers were looking straight down two hundred feet into a beautiful green valley about two miles across and a mile wide. There in the valley lay a village, the type you might see on a picture postcard but would never expect to be lucky enough to actually visit. The pasture land beyond it was grassy and hilly, and beautiful yellow bushes decorated the meadows in wild, wavy clumps.

"Those bushes! Oh, they're beautiful!" Applefeller exclaimed.

"They surely are!" Josiah Benson agreed.

"They look like yellow cotton candy!" Applefeller said. "They're everywhere! I've never seen anything like it!"

"And look at those palm trees! They must be a hundred feet high!"

"And fruit trees, sir!"

"Yes! Yes! This is the place!" Applefeller cried. "Where should we land?"

"Over there!" Josiah Benson said, pointing to a spot by the edge of the great wall of trees that surrounded the valley.

Applefeller shut off the helium nozzle, and down, down, down the great balloon fell, to a bumpy but safe landing. Quickly, Stanley and Josiah Benson untied the ropes that

attached the balloon to the cart and then hid the balloon by two palm trees. Applefeller checked the wheels and, after determining that they could still roll, put Morocco's bridle on and attached her to the front end of the cart. Instantly, the flying balloon cart was transformed back into a horse-drawn buggy.

"Hop in! Let's go!" Applefeller cried. "As my Aunt Harriet used to say: *When you're dropping in unexpectedly, you might as well be early!*"

Stanley and Josiah Benson climbed aboard, and soon they were off across a field of yellow cotton bushes on the way to the village.

"Will ya smell that air?" Josiah Benson declared. "It's as fragrant as a cow's whisker!"

After a short ride, Applefeller pulled Morocco to a halt by a shoe repair shop. A small man with bright green overalls came to the door and called to them:

"Hello! My name is Jason Lurvice.
Jason Lurvice at your service!"

There was something funny about this fellow's speech, but none of them could figure out just what. Applefeller cleared his throat and spoke: "Hello! I am John Applefeller from the town of Appleton! We've come here in search of a great pie chef, Captain B. Rollie Ragoon. Can you tell us where to find him?"

Before Jason Lurvice could answer, two men and three women stepped out of nearby shops to get a look at the strange visitors.

One of the women stepped forward:

"Today is a stunner! It shimmers and glows!
Good morning! How are you? A million hellos!"

Applefeller smiled and nodded. Just then Stanley and Josiah Benson realized something at the same time.

"They speak in rhymes!" they shouted.

"What?" Applefeller said.

"Yes! Yes sir!" Stanley said. "Look at those signs!"

Applefeller glanced above Jason Lurvice's shoe shop.

Jason Lurvice Shoe Repair
Fixes shoes like a prayer
No more rips or tears or holes
Jason Lurvice saves your soles!

"And look at that one, sir," Stanley said, pointing to a large red sign hanging from a lamppost.

IAMBIA—The Rhyming Land
Where life is never, ever bland.
We guarantee a better time
When you live your live in rhyme!

"Iambia!" Applefeller sounded out. "What does that mean?"

"I don't know, sir."

"And why does everyone speak in rhymes?" As a boy John Applefeller had always done poorly in foreign languages. Now he looked with some worry at Josiah Benson. "Captain B. Rollie Ragoon speaks normally, doesn't he?"

"He used to when I knew him," Benson said.

The Iambians had listened to this conversation as though Applefeller, Benson, and Stanley were speaking medieval Latin. Among themselves they began discussing what to do with these strange unexpected guests—the visitors with the rhyme impediment. An unfriendly few wanted them sent packing on the spot. Others suggested giving them a rhyming dictionary so they could learn to speak properly.

Josiah Benson smiled in their direction.

"I'm certain they'll be friendly if we can get 'em to catch our meanings," he said to Applefeller.

"But how? They don't seem to understand English."

"We could try rhyming, sir," Stanley offered.

"Rhyming?" Applefeller replied. "I've never rhymed before in my life!"

"Neither have I," Benson said, "but listen to this!"

Josiah Benson turned to face what was now a crowd of at least fifty Iambians. Slowly and carefully, he spoke:

"We come from a land far away as the moon,
Searchin' for Captain B. Rollie Ragoon!
We came very far on an apple balloon.
We'd sure like to see the Ragoon very soon."

A spark of recognition flared in the Iambians' eyes. Stanley stepped forward and spoke:

"We hear the Ragoon is exception'ly wise.
We'd like to see some of his magical pies."

Applefeller looked at Josiah Benson and Stanley with admiration. "Good job!" he said. "I couldn't rhyme if my life depended on it!"

The Iambians were chattering a series of quick rhymes back and forth among themselves. Then Jason Lurvice stepped forward:

"There's only one thing that we don't understand.
How did you get to our beautiful land?"

Josiah Benson reached into his coat pocket and replied:

"Finding this place was as simple as snap.
We followed the ink on this yellowy map."

He held out the map to Jason Lurvice. All the Iambians

gathered around him and tried to get a peek. In the map's right-hand corner was a note in blue ink in the Ragoon's handwriting: *Josiah: Please visit soon. Your friend, Captain B. Rollie Ragoon.*

Jason Lurvice's eyebrow hairs stood on end. No one but a true friend of the Ragoon's could have such a map.

So it was soon decided—much to the relief of Applefeller, Benson, and Stanley—that the shoe repair man himself would escort them across Iambia to the Ragoon.

11 · Captain B. Rollie Ragoon

"WHAT ARE those called?" Applefeller asked Lurvice, pointing from the cart toward a clump of yellow bushes in a nearby field.

Jason Lurvice, riding his own horse alongside Morocco, looked confused.

"You have to say it in rhymes, sir," Stanley reminded Applefeller. "He doesn't understand you."

"OK," Applefeller said. "Here goes.

"Tell me, Mr. Lurvice,
What are those yellow bushes?"

Jason Lurvice looked more confused. Stanley whispered to Applefeller: *"Lurvice* and *bushes* don't rhyme, sir."

"They don't?" Applefeller asked. "Why not?"

"Because they don't sound rhyme-like," Stanley told him.

"Oh, this rhyming business! Stanley, you ask for me."

"No, let me!" Benson said.

"I know those things aren't bumble bees.
What do ya call those yellow trees?"

Jason Lurvice's eyes lit up. He understood. He smiled at Josiah Benson and answered:

"Not bumble bees or chimpanzees
They are called boyana trees!"

"Boyana trees!" Benson exclaimed. "Well shine my shoes!"

They rode on for another half mile through a thicket of trees that opened into a wide, green meadow. Suddenly, Jason Lurvice stopped his horse. There to their left, set far back from the field under six large purple palm trees, was a small log cabin with four flower boxes beneath its front windows. A thin spiral of smoke rose from a stone chimney at the back of the cabin.

Jason Lurvice spoke:

*"The Ragoon must be home. I know you can tell it.
Breathe through your nose very deeply and smell it!"*

The four of them lifted their noses and sniffed fully. Cinnamon, flour, brown sugar, coconut, chocolate, apples, raisins, nuts, and lemon peel blended together to create an aroma so rich and creamy it felt almost possible to eat the air. For a full minute the four stayed exactly where they were with satisfied smiles on their faces. There was no question that within these walls lived a dessert-making genius.

"Jumpin' crayfish!" Benson finally declared. "Let's go in!"

He hopped out of the cart and ran to the front door of the cabin. He lifted his hand to knock but then suddenly stopped his arm in midair.

"Dancin' horsetoads! Will ya look at this!" he exclaimed.

Applefeller, Stanley, and Jason Lurvice hurried over to Benson and crouched next to him. He was staring intently at what was far from an ordinary front door. In the upper left-hand corner was a carving of an old man taking a bath in a tub of melted strawberry ice cream. To the right of the doorknob was a tiny detail of a fisherman discovering an apple pie in his net instead of a fish.

"Well, hush my puppies!" Benson cried. "Only the Ragoon would have a door like this!

"An overgrown elf with a magical mind,
   The Ragoon is a wizard—he's one of a kind!"

Jason Lurvice said.

Benson nodded and knocked. They waited a minute. There was no answer. Benson knocked again.

"Maybe he's out picking apples," Applefeller said. "It's such a nice day and . . ."

But then, suddenly, the door swung open. And standing before them was none other than the great Captain B. Rollie Ragoon.

He wore a pink-and-green checkered suit with short pants.

He wore large brown shoes with silver buckles on top.

His red crew cut pointed straight up to the ceiling as if he'd just received an electric shock.

His arms and legs twitched in different directions as if they weren't connected to the same body.

His eyebrows were red and his toenails (had they been visible through his shoes) were blue.

His pale green eyes jittered in their sockets.

His fingers twittered.

His kneecaps shook.

From under a pointy nose shone a mischievous smile.

The Ragoon, holding a large wooden spoon, squinted at his unexpected visitors, jerking his head this way and that. When his eyes finally focused upon Josiah Benson's face, his whole being took on a glow.

"Josiah! How many years has it been?
Thrilling to see you! How are you? Come in!"

"Hoppin' hogwater. It's good to see *you!*" Josiah exclaimed. The two men embraced and then shook hands warmly.

"Oh no," Applefeller murmured to Stanley, "the Ragoon speaks in rhymes too! I thought he was from our country! He must know real English!"

"He obviously does, sir," Stanley said. "He seems to understand Mr. Benson just fine."

Stanley was right. Josiah Benson and the Ragoon were talking rapidly back and forth, Josiah in English and the Ragoon in rhymes. The Ragoon clearly understood his old language. He spoke in rhymes by choice. After the Ragoon and Jason Lurvice exchanged greetings, Benson introduced his two friends.

"This here is John Applefeller," he said—"a fine apple-dessert chef! Very fine! And this is Stanley, the most trustworthy companion you'll ever find!"

Applefeller and Stanley shook the Ragoon's outstretched hand.

"A lovely place you've got here! Absolutely lovely!" Applefeller said.

"Well, let's not stand around like horses in a henhouse!" Josiah Benson exclaimed. "Invite us in!"

The Ragoon smiled.

"Josiah, you're an instant upper!
Come on in and have some supper!"

Jason Lurvice excused himself to head back to his shoe repair shop. After many thank yous from Applefeller and crew, he climbed back on his horse and cantered away across the grassy meadow.

"Captain," Benson began, coming right to the point, "this visit is more than a social call. Johnny here needs your help. He's a fine chef, but he's run out of new ideas. Could you take us into your bakery and show him a thing or two that might fire his imagination a little?"

At the mention of his bakery the Ragoon grinned, his green eyes jiggling.

"Show him my bakery? Why I'd be delighted!
Nothing else makes me a third so excited!
Nothing else makes me start crowing and shaking
Like showing good friends the desserts I've been baking!"

Just past the Ragoon's small kitchen was a pink door with three large brass handles on it. The Ragoon spun one of the handles to the left. He spun a second to the right. Then he pulled the middle handle toward him and pushed his body against the door. It opened. Applefeller, Stanley, and Josiah Benson followed him into the bakery.

An incredible sight met their eyes. Tables, stoves, and

ovens nearly filled a room as big as a basketball court. There were funnels pouring, beakers bubbling, test tubes testing, refrigerators freezing, batters battering, and bowls overflowing. Pots, pans, spoons, forks, knives, spatulas, rolling boards, butter, spices, apples, flour, and storage canisters were strewn about. Along the wall were shelves piled high with old books and ancient-looking cooking utensils.

And now that Applefeller, Stanley, and Benson were actually inside, the rich, creamy aroma they had smelled outside was even richer and creamier.

"Oh, it's wonderful," Applefeller said.

"Isn't it, sir?" Stanley agreed.

"As aromatic as a cowdog in May!" Josiah Benson said.

The Ragoon immediately started hopping from stove to stove, proudly showing Applefeller his creations and sharing with him some of his cooking secrets.

"The way to make an apple mousse
Is add eight quarts of orange juice!"

he explained as he held up a bowl of apple pudding.

"The way to make the sauces thicken
Is add the kneecaps of a chicken!"

he went on with a twinkle as he stirred a bubbly pot of

something thick and yellow that was percolating on another stove.

Applefeller and Stanley were thrilled.

"Wow," Applefeller exclaimed, "kneecaps of a chicken! Who'd have thought it?"

"And orange juice, sir," Stanley said.

"Isn't he great!" Josiah Benson beamed. "Hey, Captain, what's this over here?"

Benson's finger pointed toward a table that had on it a simple apple pie. The Ragoon joined them in three large leaps, chortling:

"Anyone can make a pie that makes a tasty mealy,
But who can make an apple pie that also speaks
Swahili?"

"Well, cover me with gravy and throw me on a turkey," Benson shouted.

"Hey, listen," Applefeller said. "I think I hear something!"

All four crouched next to the pie with their hands to their ears. Then, over the whirring and bubbling noises of desserts cooking, softly yet distinctly, they heard the pie speak in Swahili:

"Hello! I am that rare dessert who loves it when you
greet me.

But I like it even better when you pick me up and
    eat me!"

"Unbelievable!" Applefeller cried.
"Believe it! Believe it!" Benson said.
"Is it really OK to eat, sir?" Stanley asked.
The Ragoon nodded:

"Go ahead and take a bite
It said itself that it's all right!"

The Ragoon handed Stanley a knife and fork. Stanley
cut a small piece and put it in his mouth.
"Oh, Mr. Ragoon, sir," he exclaimed, happily chewing. "It's wonderful!"

12 · The Best Dessert
on Wheels

FOR THE next hour the Ragoon showed pie after pie to
his amazed visitors. He could make pies do nearly anything. There were pies that played croquet! Pies that
could tell jokes! Pies that tasted like normal pies, but
were actually made out of broiled eggplant! Applefeller's
head was bursting with new ideas.

Just when it seemed that they had seen everything, Stanley noticed something in the corner. On the floor before him was a small roller rink, ten feet across and twenty feet wide. Sitting in the center of the rink were four apple pies wearing brand new shiny roller skates and red bow-ties.

"Wow, Mr. Ragoon, sir," Stanley said. "What are these?"

"I know what they are," Josiah Benson said. "These are your roller-skating apple pies!"

"Can we see them work, Captain Ragoon?" Applefeller asked.

Applefeller, Stanley, and Josiah Benson looked over to the Ragoon, anxious for a demonstration. But the Ragoon's expression had changed. His bright smile had faded. He sniffled once or twice and then dabbed the corner of his right eye with a green paper towel. He spoke slowly, the words catching in his throat:

"If this dessert worked properly you wouldn't believe your eyes.
How I'd love to show you roller-skating apple pies!
The pies are baked,
The floor if waxed,
The wheels are screwed on straight!
But still no matter what I do the pies refuse to skate!"

"But there must be some reason they don't work good

and proper," Josiah Benson said, patting the Ragoon on the shoulder.

"Yes sir," Stanley agreed.

Collecting himself, the Ragoon explained:

"A mix-up in the recipe I haven't yet detected—
But when I get it straightened out the skates will be
*   perfected.*
Then I'll say: 'I know the way a racing driver feels.'
Then, you see, these pies will be the best dessert on
*   wheels!"*

Applefeller, Stanley, and Josiah Benson were silent for a moment. All three kept their eyes fixed on the four pies in the rink before them—four pies that indeed looked ready to roller skate. Finally, Josiah Benson broke the silence.

"Do ya think they'd work for an audience?" he suggested.

The Ragoon shrugged his shoulders and turned to a large orange machine behind him that had four levers sticking out of it. He pushed the lever nearest him. The lights dimmed. Then he pulled a long cord that hung down from the ceiling. Soon the distinct rumba of Latin music could be heard filtering into the room from two hidden loudspeakers. A man's voice started singing in the smooth mellow tones of a Hollywood film star: "Skate away with me! Skate away, I'll set you free!"

The three men and Stanley watched the pies intently. As the tempo of the music increased, the pies stood up and got ready to skate. Though it is difficult to read the facial expression of a pie, these pies looked as though they desperately wanted to perform, but couldn't.

The Ragoon sighed:

"The music gets them in the groove
But still the pies can't seem to move!"

Applefeller stared at the pies even more intently than the others, lost in his own dessert-making thoughts. After a bit, he began to rub his chin. Then, his trance broken, he turned to face the Ragoon.

"Captain Ragoon," he said haltingly, "I know you are far more talented than I, but would you object to my asking you to read me a list of ingredients that went into these pies?"

The Ragoon nodded, scratched his head, and began to reel off the list.

"I heated up the oven and I made myself a crust.
(I sprinkled on oregano to make the crust robust)
Then I took some sugar and some apples and some yeast.
And mixed them all together in a bowl that I had greased.
Then I took some raisins out of storage from the freezer,
And mixed them in the batter with a small electric tweezer.

*Then I took some toothpaste and some fresh vanilla
    custard,*
*And mixed them in the mixture with some hot Italian
    mustard.*
Then I added turtle eggs and rooster eggs and relish,
*Then something else I added, what it was I couldn't
    tellish.*
Finally, I added in some fresh Jamaican flour
And cooked it in the oven for about a half an hour.
When it came out I spread about the milk of butterflies.
That's my simple recipe for skating apple pies!"

When he was finished, the Ragoon slumped sadly into a purple easy chair in the corner of the room. But something he'd said struck John Applefeller. Nervously, though excitedly, he faced the Ragoon.

"Captain Ragoon?" Applefeller stammered. "I may not have heard correctly, mind you, but . . . well, if I wasn't mistaken, I don't think I heard you mention any Siamese flour. True, you added Jamaican flour, but I always thought that when baking a fast dessert, Siamese flour was called for."

The Ragoon looked at Applefeller and then sat up in his chair, his crew cut quivering. Applefeller took a step backward, not knowing if the Ragoon was angry or what. Then, very quickly, the Ragoon bounced onto his feet, grinning broadly.

"All the time I slaved away beside my oven cooking
I knew that there was something that I must be over-
*   looking.*
Siamese flour! Yes! I know exactly what you mean!
Siamese flour—also known as nature's gasoline!"

The Ragoon took Applefeller's hand, shook it with
great vigor, and went on:

"Isn't it a wondrous thing how funny life can be?
You came here to get my help but ended helping me!"

13 · The Ragoon's Story

"AND YOU'VE helped me too, Captain Ragoon," Applefeller said as they sat down for supper in the Ragoon's
kitchen minutes later. "More than I can say! I feel excited
about making desserts again."

"I told ya the Ragoon would inspire ya," Benson exclaimed. "And I'll bet that after ya make your own dessert, the Ragoon would be happy to show ya how to make
it not change."

The Ragoon looked at Applefeller.

"Desserts that change?
My, how strange!"

"Yes . . . well," Applefeller began, blushing. "You see—that's the other reason we came to visit. Somehow—I don't know why—my desserts always change into other things. Could you perhaps, like Josiah said, show me how to make a dessert that stays a dessert?"

"Of course he will," Benson exclaimed as the Ragoon nodded in agreement. "Then when you've got that non-changing dessert, we'll fly back to Appleton and make Sweet beg for mercy!"

At the mention of the name Sweet, the Ragoon's eyebrows twitched and his short hair stood on end.

"You know Sweet,
That awful cheat?"

"I sure do," Benson said. "He's the cowdog that's come in first place at The Worldwide Dessert Contest for eleven years in a row."

Benson went on to tell the Ragoon all the events leading up to the trip to Iambia. He related how Sweet had called the Ragoon a second-rate dessert chef. When he was finished, the Ragoon's face was beet red.

"Tell me again. Am I getting this straight?
That horrible villain called me *second-rate?"*

Benson, Stanley, and Applefeller nodded gravely. The Ragoon clenched his fists.

"Sylvester Sweet's the meanest cheat that I have ever known.
I've listened to your story. I've a story of my own!"

Applefeller, Josiah Benson, and Stanley leaned forward in their chairs. The only light in the Ragoon's small kitchen was cast by the glow of two candles that burned in the middle of the table. The Ragoon paused for a second to collect his thoughts and then began to speak.

"Many years back, how many—who knows,
Before I came here (when I still spoke in prose),
My one dream in life was to make apple pies.
But I didn't have money to buy my supplies!
But since I had loads of dessert-making knowledge,
I applied for a job at 'Dessert-Making College.'
The hiring committee was quite overjoyed.
The next thing I knew, I was duly employed!
The class that I taught was quite easy for me
(Basic Dessertmanship 323),
I knew so completely the subject I taught.
Preparing the class didn't take any thought:
How to make cupcakes to serve at a feast.
How to make pies with Bavarian yeast.
What kinds of crusts went with what kinds of dinners—
In short, it was simply a class for beginners."

The Ragoon paused for breath, and Applefeller and

the others leaned into the table a bit more closely, not wanting to miss a word.

"On the very first day of dessertmanship class
In stepped a man who looked stuffy and crass.
He said that his name was Sylvester S. Sweet!
I said, 'Glad to meet you. Now please take a seat.'
He completely ignored my most harmless request,
And wrinkled his eyebrows and puffed out his chest,
And spoke in a voice that was pompous and curt:
'Without any doubt I'm the King of Dessert,
And also the Prince of what's good in your tummy,
As well as the Captain of "Yikes that was yummy!"
I'm the best of the best of the best in the nation!
I hold thirty degrees in dessert education!' "

"So Sylvester Sweet did know who you were when I mentioned your name at the contest!" Benson exclaimed. "I knew that my meanings had special meanings to him!"
The Ragoon nodded and went on:

"I thought: 'What an odd way that is to be greeted.
I'd say that this fellow's a wee bit conceited.'
I paused, then I said when my thoughts had collected,
'If you say that your talents are wholly perfected,
Then why do you want to enroll in this college,
Since, as you say, you've no gaps in your knowledge?'
'It's true I'm the best!' Sweet replied with a cry,

'But sometimes my strudels are slightly too dry!
And so I've determined to find out just why
By observing these chefs with less talent than I!
By watching them botching their strudels and cakes,
I'll surely improve from their stupid mistakes!'
And when he was finished, that bag of hot air
Calmly adjusted his oily hair,
And looked at my eyebrows and gave me a glare,
And brushed off his shirt and sat down in my chair!
If I'd have been smart, I'd have shown him the door!
(People who sit in my chair make me sore!)
Instead I was stupid—I gave him a chance.
Besides, he had already paid in advance."

"Unbelievable!" Applefeller said.
The Ragoon took a short drink of water and continued:

"The very next morning I got out of bed
Wondering: Would Sweet be as good as he said?
One thing was certain—the man was a shnook!
But could he be also a shnook who could cook?
I walked into class feeling calm and alert,
And there stood the self-proclaimed King of Dessert.
And he said 'You will notice that here to my right
Is a triple-whipped-fudge-double-mocha delight!
This homework of mine is the peak of perfection
Made by yours truly, the Count of Confection!'

I thought, as he spoke, that he looked half-possessed.
Then he glared at my eyelids and pounded his chest.
'Prepare ye!' he shouted, 'to now be impressed!
I shall go first, since I am the best!
For I am the Prince of Perfection in Pastry!
And also the Earl of Exception'ly Tasty!'
Without any doubt he was ruder than rude
But I took a small bite and I carefully chewed!"

The Ragoon stopped for a second to take another sip of water. No one said a word. The Ragoon put down his cup and went on:

"I have to admit that I felt very glad
To find his dessert was incredibly bad.
Sweet's frightful dessert was too terribly sweet,
Sweeter than sugar that's too sweet to eat!
I took one small bite and got smithered and smuckered
Till both of my lips were unbearably puckered!
So horribly sweet was his ghastly dessert
That one of my very best students got hurt!
This unhappy pupil took only a bite
Of Sweet's triple-whipped-double-mocha delight,
And after he chewed (and I'm telling the truth)
Sweet's awful glop rotted out his front tooth!"

"Well, hush my puppies!" Josiah Benson exclaimed.

"Then how did he ever win The Worldwide Dessert Contest?" Applefeller asked. "And for eleven years in a row!"

"Yes, how?" Stanley said.

The Ragoon rose and stood by his bakery door.

"Sweet was a man who was horribly ruthless
And when his dessert let that poor fellow toothless,
He decided he had to do something but quickly
(Before his desserts made near everyone sickly).
So he followed the rule of a slithery eel
That the best things in life are the things that you steal.
And one day when I didn't have much else to do
I thought I would bake something totally new
(In truth I was actually killing some time):
So I took out some berries, I took out a lime;
I took out whatever—I didn't care what—
Some fudge and some chocolate—a ripe coconut.
And as I was tasting my raspberry treat
Who should walk in but Sylvester S. Sweet!
He stopped by to visit me while I was cooking,
Then stole my creation while I wasn't looking!

And now I find out that he's built a career,
Placed first in this contest year after year
Using a recipe stolen from me?
Why, it's simply as rotten as rotten can be!

And still he proclaims he's the King of the Cakes,
When really he's only the King of the Fakes
A faker who botches whatever he bakes!
It makes a guy angry for golly gosh sakes
To discover that he is 'Dessert's Royal Highness'
When his grade in my class was an F double minus!"

This was incredible news! It had always been agreed throughout proper dessert circles that Sylvester S. Sweet, although a vain and horrible man, was nonetheless a genius—a man with an unparalleled amount of raw dessert-making talent!

"You're joking!" Applefeller said. "You mean Sweet is a fraud!"

The Ragoon replied:

"Only the fraudiest I've ever known
He couldn't scoop out ice cream on his own!"

"I knew he was a fake! I knew he was a phony!" Josiah Benson exclaimed as he got up out of his chair. "I said so from the beginning but nobody wanted to catch my meanings!"

"Sweet is a fraud!" Applefeller repeated as if he couldn't get himself to believe it. "He's won every year with *your* dessert!"

"And not one of your better apple desserts either!"

Josiah Benson said. "It's a good thing he didn't steal your Swahili-speaking pie or your roller-skating pies!"

"It sure is, sir!" Stanley said. "Hey, wait a minute! Wait a minute! I just had an idea! What if you, Mr. Ragoon, sir, come back to Appleton with us. Then you and Mr. Applefeller can enter the roller-skating apple pies together as a team! It would be the most original dessert ever. And the Ragoon could make sure it won't change! The judges will love it! You'd be sure to win and get Sweet at the same time!"

Applefeller's eyes lit up. "That's a great idea," he said. "But is it allowed?"

"I don't see why not!" Benson exclaimed. "Stanley, you've done it again! It's a perfect idea! As perfect as a flock of swimming horsedogs! The Captain and Johnny here will be collaborators! Whatd'ya say, Captain? Come back with us to Appleton and settle with Sweet once and for all."

The Ragoon didn't know what to say.

"Please, Captain Ragoon," Applefeller pleaded. "If you don't want to win for yourself, do it for the *honor* of dessert!"

"Yes!" Stanley said. "Sylvester Sweet is giving dessert making a bad name!"

"He is! He is!" Josiah Benson said, jumping up and down for emphasis. "People everywhere think *he* is the King of Dessert! But he's not! Not no way! Not anyhow!

And anyway you've been cowdoggin' it in Iambia for long enough! It's time to come back to the real world to stand up for what really matters to ya!"

"He's right, sir," Stanley said. "What could possibly be as important as showing the world that Sweet is a fake? What could possibly be as important as dessert?"

In their excitement, Applefeller, Stanley, and Benson had gathered in a tight semi-circle around the Ragoon. The Ragoon looked at these three brave Appletonians one by one, meeting their eyes with a thoughtful stare. Then he walked to the other side of the room and searched inside himself, thinking. He was very happy living a simple life in Iambia, making desserts for his own pleasure with no contests and no pressures. But could he let down his friends? And more important, could he sit by and let Sylvester Sweet muddy the good name of desserts?

After a long pause, the Ragoon turned and spoke slowly, probably for the first time verbalizing his most deeply held beliefs:

"Some people taste a dessert and ask why,
Why does this taste make me shiver and sigh?
But I think of tastes that could sure hit the spot,
That have not yet been baked, and wonder why not?

Why not bake a pie that can speak in Chinese?
Or a pie that will bless you whenever you sneeze?

Why not bake a pie you can fly like a kite?
Or a pie to take dancing on Saturday night?

Yes, I live by a motto that's noble and true:
Don't ask what dessert can do for you!
Instead you must bake! Bake till it hurts!
And ask yourself what you can do for desserts!"

There was a deep silence after the Ragoon stopped speaking.

"That's poetry," Josiah Benson whispered finally.

"That was beautiful, sir," Stanley agreed.

"So will you come with us?" Applefeller asked. "It would be a great privilege to cook with you, Mr. Ragoon."

The Ragoon looked warmly into his three friends' eyes.

"A man cannot spend all his life on his own,
Baking desserts by himself all alone.
Where east is or west is or north is or south is
I'll travel to put Sweet's dessert where his mouth is!"

"Yippee!"

"Wonderful!"

"Welcome aboard, sir!"

The three men and Stanley shook hands and slapped backs all around the room.

"Sylvester Sweet had better start sweatin'!" Benson chortled. "Captain B. Rollie Ragoon is comin' home!"

14 · The Ragoon's Farewell

THAT NIGHT, before they went to bed, the Ragoon said to Applefeller:

"The last time I made skating pies it took about ten weeks; I had to use the most advanced of my dessert techniques. But now that we're a team, if we work without a break, I think our rolling pies should only take two weeks to make."

So every morning at five, Applefeller and the Ragoon met in the bakery. They followed the Ragoon's recipe very closely, though Applefeller did help considerably with more than one suggestion of his own. The Ragoon was particularly impressed when Applefeller discovered that an extra teaspoon of vanilla extract would help the pies accelerate around corners. And together the Ragoon and Applefeller calculated as best they could how much Siamese flour to add to the recipe. It was critical that they put in the correct amount. If they put in too much the pies might skate too fast. If they put in too little the pies might not move at all.

While Applefeller and the Ragoon were baking, Stanley and Benson packed up the Ragoon's house and got the balloon ready for the journey home.

ONE WEEK before the crew was to leave, Jason Lurvice held a farewell banquet in his shoe repair shop. Every Iambian was invited. After a sumptuous feast, Jason Lurvice rose to his feet to address them: *"Since I'm your host, I'll make a toast!"*

Jason cleared his throat and began:

"A toast to my friend Captain Rollie Ragoon,
A fellow whose heart is as big as the moon,
A fellow who bakes with a magical spoon,
And now travels east on an apple balloon.

And though your departure is inopportune
And makes me as sad as a shriveled-up prune
I hope that the day you return will be soon.
Where else do boyana trees bloom every June?

The day you come home I will hoot like a loon.
Till then, take good care, Captain Rollie Ragoon!"

"Golly gosh oh squash!" the Ragoon said, blowing his

nose in his yellow handkerchief. Everyone at the table was deeply moved. The full realization had hit home that their friend the Ragoon was really leaving to go far away. Soon, the Iambians were demanding that the Ragoon make a speech.

The Ragoon stood up, took off his festive red hat, and began:

"When in the course of making desserts,
A man must move on, though . . ."

Just then, a mailman barged into the shop.

"I struggled on through rain and hail
To bring you Applefeller's mail."

"A letter for me?" Applefeller cried.

He, the Ragoon, Stanley, and Josiah Benson all moved for the letter at the same time. Applefeller got to it first.

Curious cries echoed around the room.

"A letter?"
"Strange!"
"Let me see!"
"Postage paid or C.O.D.?"
"What's inside it? What's the dope?"
"It's got a fancy envelope!"

Applefeller's eyes opened wide and his fingers trembled as he read the letter to himself.

"Oh no! This is horrible! We'll be ruined, Ragoon! Ruined!" he moaned.

The Ragoon grabbed the letter from the shocked Applefeller.

The Iambians crowded around the Ragoon, trying to read over his shoulder. But soon they all noticed that the letter was written in standard prose.

Two guests complained:

"There's not a single rhyme in sight!
Oh, what a silly way to write!"

The Ragoon took over.

"I'll read it to you, if you'll wait,
But give me room to concentrate!
You know it takes a little time
To translate English into Rhyme."

The Iambians respectfully stepped back. The Ragoon screwed up his brow and concentrated hard. He scratched the top of his head and licked his upper lip twice.

Meanwhile Applefeller was being consoled by Stanley and Josiah Benson.

"How could he? How could he?" was all he could say.

"Hear, hear!" yelled Jason Lurvice.

The Ragoon jumped onto a chair next to Applefeller.
The room hushed as he read, or rather rhymed, the letter.

"*Sir,*
*   I am writing with little regret*
To tell you that I am extremely upset!
Remember your apple that's stuck to my face?
And your pancake that bounced me to deep outer-space?
Well, you see, I am tired of getting the hurts,
Year after year by your apple desserts!
And so I'm attempting, in cold retribution,
To somewhat revise the Dessert Constitution,
And make volume three, section five, letter C
Of paragraph forty, page seventy-three
Read, as it were, (I know it sounds awful!)
That apple desserts are from hereon unlawful!
If this change I've suggested gets ratified,
Then any dessert with an apple inside
Will not be allowed! And that, sir, means you
Will be thoroughly, uncategorically through!
Think you this punishment hasn't been earned?
Well, I'm sensitive where my good health is concerned!
Historically speaking, it would appear
The book has been shut on your dismal career.
Without you, the contest will shimmer and sparkle.

*   Good-bye and good riddance,*
*   Nathaniel H. Barkle*"

"We must leave immediately!" Applefeller bellowed. "Immediately, I tell you! Nathaniel Barkle's trying to fix it so I won't be able to enter the contest ever again! That means we won't be able to enter our roller-skating apple pies!"

"Easy, Johnny!" Benson said. "Things may not be as bad as they seem. Barkle only said he was *attemptin'* to change the dessert constitution. And you have to stay here to test-run the dessert before we go."

"No!" Applefeller insisted. "The roller-skating pies won't be ready to test-run for six more days. If we wait that long it might be too late. If we leave now we'll have time to make a brand new batch in Appleton."

"He's right, Mr. Benson, sir," Stanley said.

"*Yes!*" Applefeller shouted. "*We must make haste, not waste!*"

Applefeller stopped short and turned his head around. The Iambians looked at him in shock. Had they all heard correctly? Had Applefeller rhymed?

The Ragoon patted Applefeller on the back.

"*Haste, waste!*
It didn't come in record timing,
But Applefeller's finally rhyming!"

"No!" Applefeller shouted. "*I don't want to rhyme. There's hardly any time. Come Ragoon, this is a crime!*"

108

The Iambians cheered.

"Time, crime! Time, crime! Bravo, that's the way to rhyme!"

"If he studies and rehearses, soon he'll talk in longer verses!" Jason Lurvice commented.

"No!" Applefeller cried.

"Come, we've got desserts to bake!
The fate of apple pie's at stake!"

The Iambians gave Applefeller a standing ovation. Some threw their hats in the air.

"Applefeller's rhyming! Give the man a hand!
At last he's using language that a guy can understand."

That was all Applefeller could take. He hurried the Ragoon, Stanley, and Josiah Benson out of Jason Lurvice's shop. They found their way to the balloon—making only a quick stop to pick up Morocco—loaded their last supplies and the Ragoon's utensils, hooked up a helium canister, cut the ropes tying the cart to the ground, and flew off into the dark night—off to Appleton—to fight for what they all believed in and had staked their professional careers on: the good name of desserts.

15 · Stanley and the Judges

ON THE journey home above the Pacific, over the Hawaiian Islands, across America, Applefeller was plagued by nightmares—crazed visions of Nathaniel Barkle handing every other contestant in The Worldwide Dessert Contest the Silver Spoon while he, Applefeller, was forced to clean up the entire grounds with a small two-pronged fork. But finally, the third night after they left Iambia, Stanley guided the balloon to a safe landing in Applefeller's front yard. After they unloaded the cart, Stanley said good-bye to his friends and headed up the road for home.

"See you early tomorrow morning," Applefeller said. "Then we'll take care of stopping Judge Barkle."

"Yes sir," Stanley replied.

"He's a fine little feller," Josiah Benson remarked when Stanley was just out of earshot. "As sharp as a whip and as kind as a cowdog."

"One lucky dad
Had that lad,"

the Ragoon agreed.

Applefeller nodded. "He's a good friend," he said. "A good, good friend. Now let's get the Ragoon moved in."

STANLEY RAN the half mile to his house as fast as he could, rushed down his dirt driveway, and almost flew through the front door.

"I'm home! I'm home!" he cried.

"Stanley!" his mother exclaimed.

"Hi, Mom," Stanley said, giving her a big hug.

"I knew that apple balloon would get you there all right," his father said, patting Stanley's head. "Never doubted it for a minute."

"Tell us all about the trip," his mother said.

Stanley took a step backward.

"I'd love to, Mom," he said, "but could it wait a little while? I have to go see Judge Barkle."

"Judge Barkle?" his father said. "Why?"

"He's trying to get Mr. Applefeller kicked out of the contest," Stanley replied.

"No!" his mother gasped. "Imagine that! Well, of course you can go."

"Looks like you're just in time," his father said. "According to tonight's paper, the judges are meeting right now for the first time since last year's contest."

"Really?" Stanley said. "Why haven't they met already?"

"Says here that they couldn't," his father said, tapping the front page of the paper. "Judge Brewster McLaughlin was in Vienna developing his new Mozart sugar and George Saucery was in France interviewing Michel Deserts' cow. They only got back last night."

"I better hurry," Stanley said, racing for the door.

"Not so fast!" his mother cried.

Stanley stopped short.

"Take these," his mother said, stuffing three chocolate chip cookies into his shirt pocket. "Go get Mr. Applefeller back in that contest and then hurry home for dinner!"

"Thanks, Mom," Stanley cried.

Stanley rushed out the door, climbed on his bike, and headed out the driveway.

"And when you get back we want to hear all about your trip!" his father yelled.

As STANLEY was racing through Appleton, Judge Nathaniel Barkle and his three fellow dessert judges were just beginning their meeting in Barkle's living room. A large dusty book entitled *The Dessert Constitution—Volume III* lay on the coffee table before Barkle.

"Now look here," Barkle said, leafing through the yellowed pages. "Section five, letter C, paragraph forty, page seventy-three. All we have to do is change this one sentence that reads: 'Apple desserts are a lawful dessert' to 'Apple desserts are from hereon unlawful.' It's as easy as pie! What are we waiting for?"

"There, there, Nathaniel," Hamilton Crusthardy said. "You can't outlaw a dessert—it just isn't done."

"Quite so," snapped George Saucery. "Without apple desserts we'd be limiting the contest to non-apple desserts. Who knows what it could lead to. Next, you'll want to get rid of ice cream!"

"No." Barkle insisted. "You miss the point! Apple desserts are dangerous desserts!"

"To you perhaps," Brewster McLaughlin said, "but I rather enjoy jumping on Applefeller's pancake."

"So it was *you* I saw bouncing on it this morning," Saucery said.

"Why, yes," McLaughlin replied, "I find a morning bounce is good for the circulation."

"That pancake is a disgrace!" Barkle interjected. "A rotten nut on the hot fudge sundae of the contest!"

"Now, now," Hamilton Crusthardy said, "it's only a harmless apple-pancake trampoline. Admit it. It's John Applefeller that scares you, not apple desserts."

Upset that his fellow dessert judges were not seeing things his way, Barkle shoved *The Dessert Constitution*—

Volume III from the coffee table onto the floor and got up in a huff. But as he moved from his seat, his caramel apple accidentally hit against a desk lamp and knocked it over. Brewster McLaughlin giggled. George Saucery poked him in the ribs and said, "shhh." Barkle clenched the lamp in his fist and placed it back on the table. He faced McLaughlin, Crusthardy, and Saucery, his face bright red.

"Funny, huh?" he began. "Do you think I enjoy wearing a caramel apple? OK! I admit it! I am scared of Applefeller! I hate him! It's not easy getting hurt year after year by his desserts. Please, I beg of you. I appeal to your sense of dessert decency. For my sake. For my caramel apple's sake! Outlaw apple desserts!"

During Barkle's impassioned speech, sympathetic frowns replaced mocking smiles on the other judges' faces.

"There, there now," Hamilton Crusthardy said. "We know it hasn't been easy."

"No one said life was fair," George Saucery empathized.

"So are you with me?" Barkle asked. "No more apple desserts? No more John Applefeller?"

The three judges looked at each other and then huddled together in murmured conversation. Barkle went to the mirror to comb his hair and look at his caramel apple. He sighed—for he had long ago given up hope that he would ever be free of that brown candied fruit.

Finally, the three judges turned to face Barkle. Brewster McLaughlin stepped forward and spoke: "Nathaniel—we deeply sympathize with what you've been going through these past years. Therefore, we have decided to go along with you and outlaw apple desserts."

Barkle smiled broadly.

"Thank you," he cried. "Thank you! Safe at last! Safe at last! No more John Applefeller!'

Just then there was a knock at the front door.

"Who could that be?" Barkle asked.

"Perhaps the press wanting to interview me about my circus sugar," Brewster McLaughlin suggested.

"Doubtful," George Saucery remarked.

"Come in," Barkle yelled toward the door.

The door swung open and Stanley stepped into the room. The minute Barkle saw who it was he jumped two feet in the air and crouched behind the sofa.

"Get him away!" he shouted. "That's Applefeller's assistant. He'll hurt me somehow, I know it!"

"Relax," Hamilton Crusthardy said. "You don't have any desserts with you, do you, boy?"

"No," Stanley said.

"See," Brewster McLaughlin said, "it's perfectly safe."

"Frisk him!" Barkle demanded from behind the couch.

"Frisk him?" George Saucery said. "That's absurd!"

"Frisk him anyway!" Barkle insisted. "He may have a concealed dessert!"

McLaughlin, Saucery, and Crusthardy exchanged

glances. Brewster McLaughlin sighed and patted Stanley's shirt.

"There," he said to Barkle. "He's frisked. No desserts. Only these chocolate chip cookie crumbs in his shirt pocket."

Barkle slowly lifted his head above the sofa and scowled.

"What do you want anyway?" he demanded.

"I'm sorry to interrupt, sirs," Stanley began, "but I've come to ask you not to outlaw apple desserts. You've got to give Mr. Applefeller another chance!"

"Tough taffy, kid," Barkle said. "You got here too late."

"But Mr. Applefeller's dessert will be safe this year," Stanley said. "I guarantee it!"

"Nothing doing!" Barkle replied. "Every year his desserts have wreaked havoc! Why should this year be any different!"

"Because this year," Stanley said, "Mr. Applefeller is teaming up with Captain B. Rollie Ragoon!"

"You mean the chef that janitor was screaming about in last year's contest?" George Saucery asked.

"Yes," Stanley said. "And Captain Ragoon's the most wonderful cook in the world. He and Mr. Applefeller have teamed up to make an apple dessert that'll knock your socks off. And not only is the Ragoon a great chef, he's also one of the safest. There's no way that this dessert will change—the Ragoon would never let it happen."

"Hmmm," Hamilton Crusthardy said. "Applefeller

working with this Captain Ragoon—this changes things a bit, don't you think?"

"This changes nothing," Barkle said, now kneeling behind the couch. "All we know about this Ragoon is that he has chosen to associate himself with Applefeller, a man who makes changing desserts, and Benson, a senile janitor."

"Now, now," George Saucery said. "That's being a bit harsh. True, we don't know exactly who this Ragoon fellow is, but I'm willing to take the boy's word that he's safe."

"So am I," Brewster McLaughlin said. "I've never had anything against Applefeller anyway."

Barkle stood to his full height behind the sofa, clearly upset with the drift of the conversation.

"Hey, wait a minute," he cried. "I thought we had decided something here."

"We had," Brewster McLaughlin stated. "But if we decide something it follows that we should be able to undecide it!"

"Quite right," Hamilton Crusthardy said. "Applefeller working with this Ragoon seems safe enough."

"Absolutely," George Saucery said.

"But—" Barkle began.

"Then we're agreed," Brewster McLaughlin interrupted. "Apple desserts are hereby un-outlawed. They are now inlawed!"

"Well put!" Hamilton Crusthardy said.

Barkle looked stunned. His caramel apple seemed to droop in disappointment.

"Thank you, sirs," Stanley said. "Thank you! You won't regret it!"

"Thank you, young man, for dropping by to see us," Hamilton Crusthardy said.

"Would you like to stay for a bowl of ice cream before you go?" Brewster McLaughlin asked.

"Thank you very much, sir," Stanley replied, "but no. I've got to get home for dinner."

With those words, Stanley raced out the door, climbed back on his bicycle, and headed across town.

"CHARMING LAD," Hamilton Crusthardy said as he watched Stanley ride off.

"As charming as cold hot fudge," Barkle moped.

"Oh, cheer up," George Saucery said. "Just because you're scared of Applefeller, don't take it out on that nice boy. That Ragoon fellow will make sure Applefeller doesn't hurt anyone, you'll see."

Barkle felt his caramel apple.

"He'd better," he said. "He'd better."

16 · Sweet Pays a Visit

THE NEXT morning Stanley arrived at Applefeller's while the others were eating breakfast.

"Hi, everybody."

"Good morning, Stanley," Applefeller said. "Did you have a nice visit with your parents?"

"Oh, yes sir," Stanley replied. "They're so excited about the roller-skating pies, they're coming to the contest this year!"

"That's wonderful," Applefeller said. "But first, we have to think of some way to convince Judge Barkle to let us into the contest."

Stanley cleaned his glasses on his T-shirt. "Actually, sir," he said. "I've already taken care of that."

"What?" Josiah Benson asked.

"I went over to Judge Barkle's house last night," Stanley said. "We're back in, sirs."

"You're joking!" Applefeller said.

Stanley quickly filled them in on his meeting with the judges.

"Well, blow my nose!" Benson exclaimed. "I thought it was going to be a tough fight. But I forgot who we had on our side."

The Ragoon commented:

"Aside from having lots of heart
Stanley here is very smart."

"Thank you, Stanley," Applefeller agreed. "As usual you've saved the day. Now we can get right to work on the pies!"

And with only two weeks until the contest, Applefeller and crew had to work fast. Applefeller's kitchen wasn't big enough to fit all of the Ragoon's exotic cooking utensils, so the first few days back in Appleton were given over to converting Applefeller's large basement into a bakery.

Josiah Benson and Stanley lugged the Ragoon's many cookbooks, pots, pans, beakers, test tubes, funnels, measuring cups, pie tins, tweezers, mixing bowls, serving spoons, egg beaters, spatulas, croquet-playing pies, and Swahili-speaking pies down the creaky flight of wooden stairs.

Applefeller converted a small section of the room by the door into a roller rink. He waxed the floor, put in an old record player, and bought some Latin records for the pies to skate to.

Once everything was set up, he and the Ragoon got to work. They finished re-assembling the recipe in seven days and at last could find out what they hadn't had time to in Iambia—whether the Siamese flour would make the pies skate.

NOW THE pies were ready for testing—eight of them on the rink, each wearing a pair of shiny silver roller skates and formal red bow ties.

"The judges won't believe their eyes!
Roller-skating apple pies!"

the Ragoon chirped as he ran to the other side of the room and dimmed the lights. Applefeller went to the record player.

"Ready?" he yelled, his hand on the switch.

"Ready! But steady!" the Ragoon returned.

Applefeller put a finger on the switch and was just about to turn it when he heard a knock on the basement door.

"Who could that be?" he asked. "Stanley and Josiah are out back picking apples, aren't they?"

The Ragoon nodded.

The basement door opened.

"Hello there? Who is it?" Applefeller asked.

"Only a kindred dessert spirit. A fellow dessert chef."

Applefeller and the Ragoon exchanged troubled glances. They both recognized that voice very well. Down the stairs and into the bakery stepped Sylvester S. Sweet. He was dressed entirely in white, from his suit and tie all the way down to his socks and velvet shoes. Over the winter he had had his third front tooth capped in gold. In his right hand he held a bouquet of pink roses.

"What are you doing here, Sweet?" Applefeller said.

"I, the King of Dessert, have come on a social call," Sweet replied.

The Ragoon remarked:

"You're the King of fakery!
Leave our magic bakery!"

It was the first time the two men had met since Sweet had stolen the Ragoon's recipe for double-chocolate-fudge-raspberry-lime-coconut swirl: Sweet, the dessert fraud, and the Ragoon, the dessert genius, looked coldly into each other's eyes.

Sweet brushed his hair and checked the curl of his mustache in the diamond ring on his left index finger.

"I know that I may be unwelcome here," he began, showing his gold tooth, "but I come on a mission of peace. As the Sergeant of Scrumptious I want to show you that I can also be the Mayor of Modesty. I have come simply to wish you luck next week at the contest and to give you these lovely roses."

"That's sweet of you, Sweet," Applefeller said. "We'd ask you to stay but we're busy now."

Sweet smiled, stalling for time.

"Not even a short second for a cool glass of lemonade? It's a hot day and I have a mighty thirst."

"Forget about his mighty thirst.
He's still the worstest of the worst!
Ignore that goopy grin of his.
He's rotten still! I know he is!"

"Ah, Captain B. Rollie Ragoon," Sweet said. "How unlike you to be so rude."

"Well, one glass of lemonade couldn't hurt," Applefeller said. "As my Aunt Harriet used to say: *It's good to be polite.* And anyway, the contest is all sewn up. Our dessert this year is not only delicious, but it also moves to Latin music! Roller-skating apple pies! The judges will love it. The most original dessert ever!"

Applefeller pointed to the roller rink in the corner. Sweet's mouth dropped open.

"Think you can beat that?" Applefeller asked.

And the Ragoon said:

"Sweet, I see you're looking scared.
What dessert have you prepared?"

"Yes," Applefeller pressed. "You said you'd never enter double-chocolate-fudge-raspberry-coconut-lime swirl again. What's your new dessert?"

Sweet looked at the Ragoon blankly and then forced a wide grin.

"It's a professional secret," he stammered. "My dessert this year is so new, so original that even I am amazed by my own brilliance. If I told you what it was, you'd scrap your crazy roller-skating apple pies in two seconds and copy my idea! Worry not! I am quite sure that I will once again win the Silver Spoon."

Just then there was a loud *whack!* followed by the sound of a croquet ball hitting a wall, then rolling back in the other direction. After a pause there was another whack. And then another.

The Ragoon groaned:

"What a lousy time of day
For apple pies to play croquet!"

Applefeller, the Ragoon, and Sweet looked at the basement floor. Gliding very quickly around the room, as if on wheels, were four apple pies. Each of them was taking turns hitting one of twelve croquet balls.

"So this is the great art of Captain B. Rollie Ragoon!" Sweet mocked. "And to think that some people are deluded into thinking that you have talent!"

"Oh, be quiet, Sweet," Applefeller said.

"Don't you tell me to be quiet, you nothing. You not-anything!" Sweet was no longer looking at the floor. His steely eyes had come to rest on the eight as yet untested roller-skating pies.

"Don't start a brawl. Here comes a ball!" the Ragoon yelled.

A croquet ball came sizzling at Applefeller's feet.

"Ouch!" Applefeller yelled. "Let's stop these things!"

Boom! One of the croquet balls knocked over three cans of flour, powdering the room white.

Smash! Down fell three jars of cinnamon.

"For goodness sakery!
They're ruining my bakery!"

the Ragoon yelled, frantically pulling what he could of his crew cut.

The Ragoon and Applefeller started running in circles trying anything they could to stop the pies and croquet balls. The Ragoon grabbed a large dog-catching net off the wall and went after the pies like a fisherman netting fish. Applefeller found a long rope and quickly made a giant lasso, which he spun around his head three times and aimed at an apple pie moving very rapidly toward a shelf of pie crusts. Applefeller threw the rope and caught the pie just in time.

"Got you!" Applefeller crowed, pulling the pie toward him.

Another ball flew through the air and smashed over a

shelf of test tubes, each filled to the brim with bubbly liquids.

The Ragoon wailed:

"Not my special magic mixers!
Not my potions and elixirs!"

Sweet laughed wickedly from the corner. "Ha ha!" he cried. "This room is a dessert disaster area!"

"Quiet, Sweet. No one asked you!" Applefeller yelled.

Boom! A shelf of mixing bowls toppled down.

"Ragoon, we've got to stop these pies!"

"Good luck, Applefeller," Sweet roared. "They're ruining your entire bakery!"

Applefeller glanced around the room. Sweet was right—the pies had to be stopped.

"Come on, we aren't defeated yet. I've got another in my net!" the Ragoon shouted.

Applefeller ran to the other side of the room, tracking the two remaining pies which were zooming past side by side. Any second now . . . carefully . . . he spun his lasso a few times, squinted, licked his upper lip, took aim. . . . But then, out of the corner of his eye he saw Sylvester Sweet inching his way toward the roller-skating-apple-pie rink.

"Hey! Get away from there!" Applefeller yelled.

The next thing Applefeller knew he was doing a backward somersault. The two pies he was going to lasso had smashed into his feet and flipped him into the air.

"Whoa!" he yelled. "Stop!"

But Applefeller kept flying head over heels until, with a loud crash, he smacked into a pyramid of apples and fell to the floor.

The two pies sailed onward to hit the Ragoon square in the face, knocking his long bony body into a pile of pie tins. With no moving pies to hit them, the croquet balls gradually lost speed and came to a halt. But great damage had been done to the bakery. Shelves and tables were overturned. Spices, books, and utensils were spilled all over the floor.

The Ragoon got up slowly, wiping pie off his face. He ran over to Applefeller and helped him to his feet.

"While you were flipping up in space
I stopped the pies—with my face!"

the Ragoon informed him.

Applefeller looked around the bakery.

"What a mess!" he cried.

Then he looked toward the door.

"Where's Sweet!?!" he cried.

The Ragoon rushed to the other side of the room. He turned back to Applefeller, his face white.

"Sweet will stoop to any level.
He's as rotten as the devil!
He took what's sure to win first prize,
All our roller-skating pies!"

17 · The New Dessert

MOMENTS AFTER Sweet had pulled away in his white sports car, Stanley and Josiah Benson ran down the stairs to the basement.

"What happened here?" Benson asked.

"Sweet stole our pies!" Applefeller cried. "He stole our pies!"

"Oh no, sir," Stanley said, looking at the empty corner where the pies had once stood.

"That stinkin' dogcat!" Benson bellowed.

The Ragoon agreed:

"Sweet is even worse than that
He's a worn-out dog-cat mat!"

"Let's go after him," Benson said.

"No, we can't!" Applefeller moaned. "Sweet's no fool! I'm sure he's already announced to the papers that's he's entering the roller-skating pies. No one would ever believe he's stolen the roller-skating pies from us, just like no one would ever believe he stole the swirl from the Ragoon! His reputation is too great! He'll enter our pies and win. It's that simple!"

Applefeller kicked a turned-over flour canister and sat down on the stairs.

"Then we'll have to make a new dessert that's even better than roller-skating apple pies," Stanley said matter-of-factly.

"What?" Applefeller asked, standing back up. "Be serious! What could possibly be better than roller-skating apple pies? And anyway, those pies took weeks to make. Even if we had a new dessert we haven't enough time."

"Well, I don't know about that," Josiah Benson said. "We do have four days."

"That's right," Stanley agreed. "What do you think, Captain Ragoon, sir?"

The Ragoon tugged on his crew cut and spoke:

"There is one special apple pie
That I would like a chance to try.
If Johnny helps me out we might
Win the Silver Spoon all right."

Excitedly, the Ragoon explained his idea for a new dessert—a dessert that, if it worked, could beat even roller-skating apple pies.

"I like it," Benson said when the Ragoon was finished.

"Me too," Stanley added.

All eyes turned to Applefeller. But Applefeller shook his head. "It's too crazy—even for the Ragoon to pull off."

The Ragoon held Applefeller by the shoulders:

"This dessert could be a dream
If we make it as a team."

Applefeller looked into the Ragoon's eyes—the eyes of the man who had taught him so much. "Well," he said. "If you *really* think we can do it, maybe it is worth a try. I mean, we can't just sit around here for four days doing nothing, right?"

So they got to work again. They cleaned up their bakery. They punished the croquet-playing apple pies by making each of them write "I will not play croquet indoors" five hundred times on a blackboard.

Then the baking began.

For four days the Ragoon, Applefeller, Josiah Benson, and even Stanley worked almost around the clock.

The morning of the contest Applefeller fretted: "What if they taste bad? What if they crash?"

"Have a little faith, sir," Stanley replied, as they loaded up Morocco's cart.

"But we haven't even taken them on a test flight yet," Applefeller persisted.

*"Calm yourself—don't get unglued.
Maintain a winning attitude,"*

the Ragoon replied.

"You're as jumpy as a rooster in a cowhouse!" Josiah Benson declared.

"I know I'm jumpy," Applefeller said, "but whenever I think of Sylvester Sweet entering our roller-skating pies it makes me crazy! And our dessert is so risky!"

The Ragoon smiled.

*"The judges won't believe their eyes!
An apple pie that also flies!"*

"They're gonna work!" Josiah Benson cheered, jumping up and down on the cart. "I can feel it in my whiskers!"

"Well, if you feel it in your whiskers, maybe . . ." Applefeller said, encouraged by his friend's enthusiasm. "Flying apple pies! As my Aunt Harriet used to say: *Never assume something won't work unless you're really sure it won't work.*"

"Now you're talking, sir!"

"Stanley," Applefeller continued, "are you positive you've packed everything?"

"It's all here, sir, including the apple pie you made for our lunch."

"Good," Applefeller said. "As my Aunt . . ."

"Enough of this chit-chatty-chitter-chatter!" Benson interrupted. "Let's get goin'!"

Applefeller, the Ragoon, Benson, and Stanley climbed into the cart. Applefeller took the reins and Morocco broke into a trot. And they were on their way to the Twelfth Annual Worldwide Dessert Contest—three men, one boy, their horse, and their flying apple pies.

PART

THREE

18 · Before the Contest

THE ROAD to the stadium was jammed with honking buses and cars, for word of Sylvester Sweet's roller-skating apple pies had created a sensation. Anything to do with the champion was selling like milkshakes.

Vendors on roller skates were hawking miniature replicas of what people guessed roller-skating apple pies might look like. Vendors dressed as roller skates were selling apple pies; vendors wearing Sylvester Sweet masks were selling roller skates.

And that was just the tip of the ice cream cone.

There were Sylvester Sweet pens, Sylvester Sweet flashlights, Sylvester Sweet hats, posters, T-shirts, buttons, place mats, sheets, pillowcases, coasters, buttons, belts, socks, shoelaces, hair spray, bookmarks, long underwear, mustache combs, and tweezers.

"Get your Sylvester Sweet pillowcases!" one vendor yelled. "Every time you sleep, put your head on the great dessert genius!"

"Sylvester Sweet socks here," cried another. "Put Sweet on your feet!"

Word had reached the crowd that a man named "Ragoon" was helping Applefeller this year. As Applefeller and crew made their way up to the contestants' entrance gate, several people shouted out:

"Hey, isn't the guy with the red crew cut that weirdo Ragoon?"

"Yeah. And get this. They say he makes magic desserts!"

"Magic desserts? That's a good one!"

"Well, if he does, why doesn't he make a dessert that will teach him how to dress?"

At this last comment the Ragoon spun his head around. Although he was hurt that the crowd didn't believe he could make magic desserts, he was even more upset with the comments about his clothes. He didn't think there was anything at all odd in wearing orange and green checked pants, a blue and violet dress shirt, and a yellow bowtie. And that morning he had taken extra care in the combing of his red eyebrows.

Soon Applefeller directed the cart away from the crowd, pulling up in front of the dessert registrar. In the registrar's right hand was a pen, in his left, a bowl of cherry mango fudge ice cream. He looked over his pad of paper at Applefeller.

"Oh! You again?" he giggled.

"Yes me!" Applefeller said.

"Dessert?" the registrar inquired.

"Flying apple pies," Applefeller said.

"Flying apple pies?" the registrar exclaimed. "Oh, I get it! You mean an apple pie that changes into a 747!"

"Very funny!" Applefeller said. "Just tell us where to set up please."

"Yes, here we are," the dessert registrar said as he peered through some papers, "same place as last year. Row three, position 333, next to your apple-pancake trampoline and right next to Sylvester Sweet."

Morocco pulled the cart through the short tunnel and up the incline into the bright sunlight of the dessert grounds.

The inside of the stadium was twice as frantic as the outside. Even now, half an hour before the contest was to begin, the fans were standing up, screaming. From the left corner of the bleachers hung a pair of gigantic plastic roller skates; on the other side, a plastic balloon skate key.

"Hoppin' horse-ants!" Josiah Benson exclaimed. "Look at all these people! They'll make more garbage than a herd of messy toadhogs!"

Benson looked toward the right-hand corner of the field. There stood forty large empty garbage bins—forty bins that would be filled to the brim with trash by the end of the day. At the same time, Applefeller looked toward his apple-pancake trampoline and sighed. There was a line of three hundred people waiting for a pre-contest bounce. As they drew closer, he saw that Brewster

McLaughlin, the sugar expert, was at the front of the line!

"Forget about that pancake, sir," Stanley said as they arrived at row three, position 333, "you're going to teach everyone here a thing or two by the end of the day."

Applefeller smiled and patted Stanley on the head. Then he turned his back to the trampoline and got to work setting up. As Applefeller and crew laid out their four flying pies on the dessert table, they noticed several familiar faces. Michel Deserts, Princess Irma Frostina, and Reginald Coco and Razine were all back for another try at the Silver Spoon. And reporters swarmed the field like a gang of hungry bees, interviewing anyone they could. Suddenly Applefeller found himself surrounded by television cameras—and a familiar reporter.

"OK Applefeller, give it to us and give it to us straight. We're both adults here, so I'm gonna just come right out and say it. You're a failure. Why do you return here year after year? Do you enjoy being laughed at?"

Applefeller stood bravely in front of the microphone without blinking.

"I return here every year," he said, "because I believe in desserts, especially apple desserts. As my Aunt Harriet used to say: *It's fine to fail so long as what you fail at is worth the effort.*"

"Hmmm . . ." the reporter said, "Your Aunt Harriet sounds like a weirdo. Is she a weirdo? Are you a . . ."

Applefeller turned bright red. His left eye twitched.

"My Aunt Harriet was the finest woman to ever live

on this earth!" he blurted. "You can say what you will about me, but you leave her out of it!"

"OK, OK," the reporter said. "No Aunt Harriet. I'm getting it straight."

The reporter turned to the Ragoon. Television cameras and bright lights zoomed in on his face.

"Mr. Ragoon, give us the scoop. Josiah Benson says you're good—darn good. Are ya really that good? Are you as good as Sylvester Sweet is good? Are you as good as you once were? Are you as good as you will be in the immediate future? When were you better? Now or then? When were you worse? Then or now?"

The Ragoon was angry at how rudely Applefeller and Aunt Harriet had been treated. He decided to confuse the reporters with one of his most dazzling rhymes. He looked straight into the camera and then spoke very quickly.

"How good am I? Well, let me see.
Just as good as good should be.
Years ago I thought I could
Never, ever be as good
As I am now, but then again
Maybe I was better then!
And if that's true, I've been a dunce
To get less good than I was once.
But if it's true I once was worse,
I'm getting worse in reverse.

And so you see I'm in a jam.
It's hard to tell how good I am.
Then or now, now or then?
Repeat the question once again?"

All the reporters were dumbstruck. This was the most bizarre answer ever. Applefeller grinned.

Josiah Benson broke the silence.

"If you nosy fellers wouldn't mind, we have to set up our dessert, if ya catch my particulars!"

The reporters willingly collected their cameras and went off to look for a contestant who would supply less confusing answers.

"Well," Applefeller said, "let's get ready."

But as they turned toward their dessert table, a voice boomed, "Applefeller!"

It was Judge Barkle.

"Sir?" Applefeller stammered.

Barkle seemed to have aged considerably. His face was wrinkled. His caramel apple was darker brown.

"Applefeller," Barkle said, "I am here to say one and only one thing."

"Yes sir?" Applefeller said.

"Applefeller, I'm sick and tired of getting hurt by your desserts. The only reason you're in the contest this year is because this kid showed up and convinced the other judges that that crackpot Ragoon would keep your dessert from changing. But let me warn you, if I get injured in any way at this contest, and I mean if I even so much as stub my toe, I am holding you personally responsible and throwing you out for good no matter what the other judges say!"

"Is that fair, sir?" Stanley asked.

"Don't talk to me about fair, son," Barkle snapped. "Applefeller, you are a disgrace! The stale crust on the Boston cream pie of this contest!"

"But it's not right!" Josiah Benson said.

"I'll worry about what's right, mister," Barkle grimaced. "You just worry about your trash!"

Barkle took a crumpled candy wrapper out of his pocket and dropped it on the ground.

"Get busy," he said.

Josiah Benson looked at the white and brown wrapper in front of him. He had no choice. He strapped his garbage bag onto his shoulder, stooped down to pick up the paper, and headed away through the dessert grounds.

Applefeller, the Ragoon, and Stanley watched him go.

"Good-bye, Mr. Benson, sir," Stanley said.

Benson turned.

"I'll be back when you get judged!" he said.

Applefeller and the Ragoon waved.

Barkle started to walk away. Before he had taken more than one or two steps, the Ragoon stepped forward.

"But sir, it really isn't right
To blame us if . . ."

143

"Enough!" Barkle shouted.

The Ragoon's green eyes opened and closed. He hadn't been cut off mid-rhyme in many years.

"I decide what's right around here! Get it?" Barkle's caramel apple reflected the sun and shone brightly. "If I get hurt in any way, Applefeller, you're through!"

Barkle turned and stalked back to the judges' stand.

19 · The Opening Ceremonies

"I KNOW we haven't come any other year," Stanley's mother said as she and her husband walked into the dessert stadium, "but those flying pies sound like such a charming idea."

"Oh yes," her husband replied. "And this Ragoon fellow will be worth seeing. Stanley tells me he's a wonderful conversationalist."

As Stanley's parents took their seats in the bleachers, the four judges moved solemnly onto the judges' stand. The opening ceremonies were about to begin. All of the chefs, spectators, and reporters were in place. There was only one person missing—Sylvester Sweet. Everyone was so busy straining to catch a first glimpse of him that no one noticed the green and gray shape flying lower and lower above the dessert grounds. But finally, people began to look up.

"What's that?"

"It's a giant flying cockroach!"

"No! It's Sylvester Sweet!"

Sweet and Tuba were being lowered onto the field by a green helicopter. Four mighty ropes hung down from the helicopter and were strapped underneath Tuba's body. Tuba was swaying gently back and forth, so calm he almost looked bored. Sweet was beaming, obviously pleased with the stir his entrance was making. As they swung closer to the ground, spectators in the upper bleachers shouted out:

"Why there must be thirty people on the back of that elephant!"

"Who are they?"

"The only one I recognize is Dentina!"

"All the others have musical instruments with them!"

"No!"

"Yes! Look!"

Perched on Tuba's back, behind Sweet and Dentina, were thirty men and women carrying saxophones, trumpets, trombones, clarinets, drums, guitars, violins, cellos, xylophones, bassoons, French horns, flutes, piccolos, and zithers. Then, above the loud whir of the helicopter propellors, the band started playing a forceful march.

The crowd was overwhelmed. Everyone except Stanley's parents stood up and cheered. Sweet was pulling off one of the greatest entrances in dessert contest history.

"Well, cover me with roosters and throw me in the henhouse!" Josiah Benson muttered from among the garbage bins.

The sound of the helicopter was deafening now. Many people held their ears as the great green machine set Tuba down in front of the judges' stand. Sweet waved good-bye to the helicopter pilot and stood up between Tuba's ears. He spread his arms above his head, basking in the crowd's cheers. Then, as some of them continued playing, the rest of the band began singing with great feeling:

Sylvester Sweet, Dessert King!
Tell me if it's true.
Is there any way on earth
That I can be like you?

Sylvester Sweet—Dessert King!
Brilliant from your birth!
But you're the King of everything
That's sweet upon the earth!

The band members sang the song through three times and then ended with a loud, dramatic crescendo.

"Dentina," Sweet commanded. "Assist in my descent! The ladder!"

147

Dentina handed a ladder to a musician who placed it against the right side of Tuba's body. Sweet climbed down.

"Continue!" Sweet said.

Tuba moved through the crowd and positioned himself by Applefeller's pancake. The musicians clambered off the elephant and set up their stands.

Nathaniel Barkle took the microphone and made an announcement:

"Ladies and gentlemen, I give you Sylvester Sweet!"

Sweet quickly checked his hair in the reflection from the ruby ring on his left thumb, and then adjusted one curl behind his left ear.

"Excellent! I look simply perfect!" he declared, walking over to Nathaniel Barkle and taking hold of the microphone.

"Thank you, fellow dessert lovers!" he began. "This is your King of Dessert speaking. As you all know, this year I am entering the world's first roller-skating apple pies!"

The crowd let out an enormous cheer. Sweet stretched the skin on his face as far as it could go in a wide thankful smile.

"Thank you!" he said. "It *is* overwhelming to be near me, isn't it? To assist me this year I have brought along the Sylvester Sweet Dessert Band. These fine musicians have the historic opportunity of playing the Latin music for my pies to skate to! In exchange, all they have asked for is the chance to enter my private baking chamber to touch some of my ingredients."

The crowd cheered again. From the other side of the field Tuba let out a loud honk. John Applefeller shook his head in disbelief.

Sweet continued with his opening speech. As usual, it was filled to the brim with bad taste. Then he stood close by as an eight-year-old boy from Appleton Elementary scooped out the traditional first scoop of ice cream. When this brief ceremony was finished, Sweet left the stage to join Dentina, Tuba, and the musicians.

Nathaniel Barkle spoke into the microphone:

"Let The Worldwide Dessert Contest begin!"

20 · Sweet and Applefeller

APPLEFELLER DRUMMED his fingers nervously together.

"How can I help it if Barkle twists an ankle or gets a bloody nose?" he moaned, thinking of what the judge had said to him before Sweet's entrance. "It'll be sure to happen. I'll be kicked out forever!"

"Don't be so blue, sir," Stanley said. "What would your Aunt Harriet have said?"

Applefeller paused a minute.

"I don't know!" he cried.

Stanley and the Ragoon were quiet. If Aunt Harriet

had nothing to say about something, the situation was certainly serious.

Applefeller pointed at Sweet and the roller-skating apple pies across the way.

"Look at that!" he said. "That's the dessert we should be entering!"

The Ragoon spoke up:

"Calm yourself! Don't go berserk!
We don't know if those pies will work!
We don't know if those pies will skate,
For pies are hard to navigate."

Applefeller walked over to the tree stump he'd sat on the year before.

"It's true we didn't test them," he said, "but how do we know that Sweet hasn't tested them in the last four days? And what about our flying pies? It's not as if we've tested them either!"

Applefeller, unconsoled, leaned his chin on the palm of his hand and sighed.

Just then Sweet caught a glimpse of him.

"Hey, Applefeller!" he jeered. "How does it feel to be the Lord of Last Place?"

The Ragoon held Applefeller's shoulder:

"Ignore his evil vicious squawking.
Our dessert will do our talking!"

150

But Applefeller could not contain himself.

"Why, you miserable liar," he cried. "*Everyone* here knows that you stole those roller-skating apple pies from the Ragoon and me from out of *my* basement!"

There was a sudden deep silence. Cameras stopped clicking, spectators stopped cheering, reporters stopped talking, chefs stopped preparing, and the judges stopped judging. Everyone looked at Applefeller.

"Oh no," Stanley's mother said to her husband. "No one believes him!"

"Oh no, sir," Stanley said to Applefeller. "No one believes you!"

Applefeller, realizing that Stanley was right, stood with his mouth half open. Sweet, sensing his advantage, took his time in responding. His grin slowly turned into a full-fledged mocking guffaw.

"You . . . You? You??? Me steal from you?" Sweet began. "Did you hear that ladies and gentlemen? Applefeller, Mr. Dessert Failure himself accusing *me*, the King of Dessert, of stealing from him! It's almost too outrageous to be believed! If it wasn't so funny, I'd be angry!"

Sweet began laughing so hard his new gold tooth came loose. Dentina rushed to put it back in place with a large monkey wrench.

Some unruly fans yelled:

"Give it up, Applefeller!"

"Nice try, jerk!!"

"Go take your Ragoon for a walk!"

Applefeller kicked the tree stump.

"Ouch," he yelled, hopping up and down on one foot.

"Good-bye, Applefeller!" Sweet said. "After you and the Ragoon lose to my brilliant roller-skating apple pies, maybe you'll do everyone a favor and retire! You are a 'never-will-be-ever-in-a-million-centuries-anything-worthwhile-at-all-to-anyone.' "

As Dentina wiped off Sweet's brow with a wet cloth, the Ragoon put his arm around Applefeller's shoulder, helping him regain his balance.

"I can't stand it!" Applefeller seethed. "All the world thinks that Sweet has created the swirl *and* the skating pies! Nothing we can say will convince them otherwise! Ragoon, tell me. How can you stand it? How can you stand having to be quiet around that villain Sweet?"

The Ragoon glared at Sweet and smiled grimly:

"Only by imagining the look across his face
When he sees our apple pies orbiting in space."

21 · A Very Close Contest

As USUAL, the judging took all day. The four men plowed through contestant after contestant like a mighty monster leaving a trail of broken hearts in its wake. All day long, Applefeller, the Ragoon, and Stanley could hear their voices echoing down the field.

Judge Barkle: "Historically speaking, I would compare this dessert to a leather shoe eaten by migrant workers during the Depression!"

Or Hamilton Crusthardy: "Let me let you in on a little secret. When baking a cake it is much better to use an oven! I have found that actually *cooking* a cake makes for a less runny texture!"

Stanley's parents were very proud that their son was part of a contest with such high standards. Only a lucky, talented few chefs were judged favorably. By late afternoon, with only Sweet's and Applefeller's desserts left to be considered, Michel Deserts and Reginald Coco were tied for first place. George Saucery had been especially impressed with the triple ripple in Deserts' ice cream. And Brewster McLaughlin was enchanted with Reginald Coco's combined use of basket sugar and ball sugar. If neither Sweet nor Applefeller could beat these two excellent chefs, Deserts and Coco would be competing for the Silver Spoon in a sudden-death taste-off.

Sadly, Irma Frostina had once again done poorly. At this point in the contest she was in 905th place. She was outraged.

"Zes is ridiculous!" she cried. "I travel all the vay from Germany for zes? I vant to vin! Zes is the last straw! I vill convince the judges!"

With those words Frostina drew her red veil over her face and walked alluringly up to Nathaniel Barkle.

"Say there, Nathaniel, darling," Frostina cooed. "Oh—you are *so* attractive. Not many men have the imagination to vear an apple on their face! How clever you are!"

"I say . . ." Barkle responded. "I never knew you liked my apple."

"And you," Frostina said, sidling up to Brewster McLaughlin, "personally I like a man who isn't afraid to eat a good meal. It builds character."

"Well thank you, Princess!" McLaughlin said, patting his belly. "Not enough people appreciate the value of being grossly overweight!"

"You're so right," Frostina breathed.

She next wiggled close to Hamilton Crusthardy.

"Ohhh!" she said, gently rubbing his chin. "Darling, vat muscles! Vat a jaw! It's the type of mouth a girl *dreams* about!"

"Well, " Crusthardy said, trying to be modest, "it is muscular!"

"It certainly is, darling."

Finally, Frostina made her way over to George Saucery.

"You don't fool little old me one bit," she cooed. "You try to be so serious, but underneath you're just a cuddly baby lamb!"

Here Princess Irma A. Frostina went too far. She'd

forgotten that George Saucery was a man of great dessert integrity.

"I am no such thing!" Saucery stated. "Underneath I am even more serious than I am overneath!"

Frostina drew away. Saucery turned to the other judges.

"Need I remind you gentlemen what we are here for? Our attention to the tasting of desserts must not be diverted!"

At this the other three judges snapped out of the spell Frostina had woven about them.

"Quite right!" Barkle agreed.

"Indeed!" McLaughlin confirmed.

"Yes!" Crusthardy said.

"Curses!" Frostina moaned.

She knew she'd been defeated for another year.

"I vant the Silver Spoon! I vant the Silver Spoon! Vy can't I ever vin the Silver Spoon?"

"Because your desserts stink!" George Saucery sputtered. "Personally, I'd rather eat fried mud. Now get away!"

"*Ahhhh!*" Frostina threw herself, sobbing, at the other three judges' feet. "Please! Please! *Please!* I vant the Silver Spoon!"

"Come now, Frostina!" Crusthardy said. "Stop licking my shoes! I can't concentrate!"

"Police! Police!" McLaughlin cried as Frostina tried unsuccessfully to put her arms around his fat waist.

Two policemen ran over, and so it was that, for the

eighth year in a row, Princess Irma A. Frostina was carried, screaming, off the dessert grounds.

22 · Roller-skating Apple Pies

BUT NOW the big moment had arrived. The roller-skating apple pies were about to be tasted.

The judges stepped up to Sweet's table.

"So these are your new creations, are they?" Barkle inquired as he looked at what appeared to be eight very ordinary-looking pies, except that they wore black tuxedos and red bowties and had roller skates carefully attached to their bottoms.

"Yes!" Sweet responded. "I think you will find them to be most delectable. Most entertaining!"

Across the way Applefeller clenched his fists.

"It's *our* dessert, Captain," he muttered.

"Shhhhhh, sir," said Stanley.

The Ragoon patted Applefeller's back consolingly.

"When our dessert has taken off and circled through the sky
 Sylvester Sweet will have to eat a slice of humble pie."

"When do we taste them?" Hamilton Crusthardy asked. "Before or after they skate?"

"After, after!" Sweet grinned. "What you are about to see is the most incredible dessert sensation ever in the history of the Western world. When this demonstration is complete, I will be known not only as the King of Dessert, but also as the Diety of Dessert!"

"We'll be the judges of that!" George Saucery intoned.

"On with it. On with it," added Brewster McLaughlin.

"Very good!" Sweet said. "*Dentina!* My baton!"

Dentina picked a white baton off the dessert-tasting table and handed it to Sweet. Sweet turned toward the judges.

"You may not be aware of this, gentlemen, but my elephant, Tuba, is a beast of many talents. Besides serving as my pet, spiritual advisor, bodyguard, and faithful friend, Tuba is also a musician. Maestro—if you please!'

Tuba reached out with his trunk, took the baton from Sweet, and kneeled on his back legs in front of the band.

"You may begin upon my signal!" Sweet said. "Dentina! Help me with the pies!"

Sweet turned to the pie skating rink. Dentina handed the pies to him one by one. Sweet arranged them in a circle.

"Yes! Yes! Prepare to witness greatness!"

"We're quite prepared, Sweet," McLaughlin said. "On with the show!"

The bleachers near Sweet were overflowing with spectators who had pushed and shoved their way from other parts of the stadium to get a closeup view of dessert

157

contest history. Packed together like jelly beans, these dessert fans barely had space enough to breathe. The swarm of reporters was kept at bay behind a large police barricade to the left of Sweet's dessert.

The dessert grounds grew so quiet you could hear hot fudge bubble. The only sound was an electric buzzing in the air. Stanley's parents leaned forward in their seats.

Sweet signaled to Tuba. Tuba raised his baton high and at the mighty downward sweep of his trunk the musicians began playing a rhythmic bossa nova in steady 4/4 time. Tambourines shook, clarinets rang, saxophones blared, violins sang, and drums rumbled.

"Well, let's see some action!" Brewster McLaughlin said. "The band sounds fine, but why aren't the pies moving yet?"

"Soon! Soon!" Sweet oozed.

Tuba waved his baton and increased the tempo of the music. One of the band members stood up and started

to sing: "Roller-skating apple pies! Skate away with me!"

"Yes! Yes!" Sweet yelled.

And then, very slowly, the pies inched clockwise. The crowd blinked. The faint *click-clack* of wheels rolling on a rink filled the air.

"I'm seeing things!" yelled one fan.

"It's a miracle!" said a policeman.

"It's a trick! It's done with wires!" cried someone else.

"I assure you, there are no wires!" Sweet said.

The pies started skating faster. The steady whir of spinning skate wheels grew louder and louder.

"Fascinating," Hamilton Crusthardy observed.

"This is a fine dessert!" Judge Barkle said.

"That was *our* dessert!" Applefeller said. "And look at them! I knew that Siamese flour would work!"

"Quiet, sir," Stanley said.

The Ragoon watched silently, patiently waiting for the chance to fly their pies.

"Skate away with me forever!" the singer crooned. Tuba waved his baton faster still. The pies kept accelerating. Then, in a flash, the eight pies stopped skating separately and paired up, making four couples.

"Incredible! How original!" Hamilton Crusthardy exclaimed.

"Rather impressive," George Saucery admitted.

Faster and faster the pies moved! Oohs and aahs echoed up and down the dessert grounds. The band played faster and louder. Marimbas, castanets, and bongo drums joined in. Spectators, reporters, and policemen alike clapped their hands and swayed their hips to the steady driving beat. One fan got so carried away that he jumped out of the bleachers onto the field and did a little jig, waving his arms above his head and wiggling his belly.

Then Dentina took out a large megaphone and led the crowd in a cheer:

"Rol-ler skate! Rol-ler skate!"

The bleachers shook as the the fans rocked back and forth, chanting, hypnotized.

Above the din, voices of excited reporters could be heard:

"This is unbelievable! Talk about original! Sweet has redefined dessert as we know it. He has made a dessert as we don't know it!"

Sweet himself was loving every second. Grinning widely, rubbing his emerald rings, brushing back his hair, he positively sparkled. He gestured to Dentina with his pinky, and she led the crowd in another cheer:

"Sylvester Sweet—Dessert King!"

The crowd picked up the chant as the pies skated faster and faster, now in figure eights.

"This is a great show!" McLaughlin said as he clapped his hands above his head.

"It *is* wonderful," Judge Barkle agreed. "But when do we get to taste these pies?"

"Momentarily," Sweet replied. "Maestro! Cease the music!"

Tuba nodded his big head and stopped waving the baton. The band ended in a mighty blast with the two trumpeters blaring piercing high notes. The singer belted one final "Skate away with me!" Spectators, reporters, and judges cheered.

Sweet bowed and then gestured toward Tuba and the band. Tuba stood up on his hind legs, waved his trunk back and forth, and let out a loud honk. Sweet pointed toward the band members who bowed with self-satisfied grins on their faces. Sweet checked his hair in a ruby ring on the index finger of his left hand and then faced the judges.

"Now then, you can taste my brilliant dessert!" he said.

"We'd love to taste your dessert, Sweet," Hamilton Crusthardy answered. "But the pies appear to be still moving!"

23 · "Stop Those Pies!"

"WHAT!" Sweet cried.

He looked over his shoulder and into the rink. The pies were indeed still roller skating in figure eights.

"Stop! Stop!" Sweet yelled.

But the pies didn't stop. They went faster and faster.

"What's wrong?" George Saucery asked.

"Wrong? Wrong? Nothing's wrong!" Sweet said, improvising frantically. "It seems that I have made these pies *too* expertly. So brilliant are these pies that they have minds of their own, and being the world's only *thinking* apple pies, they need to skate for another minute collecting their thoughts, as it were—before they feel ready to be tasted."

"You mean you *cannot* stop the pies?" George Saucery asked with an upward turn of one eyebrow.

"Of course I can!" Sweet retorted.

He walked to the edge of the rink and yelled at the pies, now moving so fast they were hard to see.

"*Stop skating right now!* This is your King of Dessert speaking, and *I command you to stop at once!*"

But the pies kept circling. TV cameramen began running their film extra fast in an effort to keep pace with the ever speedier skaters. Sweet turned back to the judges and grinned sheepishly. Then he jumped over the railing into the rink and started chasing after the pies, trying anything he could think of to make them stop.

The crowd started laughing.

"What's going on here?" Barkle barked.

Nearby, the Ragoon tapped Applefeller on the shoulder.

"Without a doubt that Siamese flour
Gave those pies some extra power!"

Applefeller slowly began to smile.

"Yes," he chuckled, "I guess we must have added a bit too much."

And to say these pies had "extra power" was an understatement. The pies were in overdrive—out of control.

"Stop those pies!" McLaughlin boomed. "We must taste your dessert!"

"Right away!" Sweet gasped, now crawling around the rink trying to block the pies with his body. "Tuba! Dentina! *Help me!*"

Dentina leaped those railing. But her high-heeled shoes gave her little traction on the roller rink surface and she tripped and knocked Sweet flat on his back. Then Tuba lumbered over to help, but unfortunately for Sweet, Tuba lumbered right through the rink's railing, knocking out a large hole.

"Tuba! Bad boy!" Sweet cried. "Bad Bishop of Beasts!"

Sweet threw his body in front of the hole in an effort to block the pies before they could skate out of the rink. But he was too late. Before you could say "rainbow sprinkles" the pies rushed through the hole and started spinning recklessly through the dessert grounds.

"Ahhhh!" Sweet cried. *"Stop those pies!"*

The crowd was screaming.

"Nice dessert, Sweet!"

"Sweet's no Dessert King!"

Reporters gushed into their microphone: "Sweet's pies escape! They're skating out of control and could be dangerous!"

The pies rolled by dessert tables, through reporters' legs, and by the judges' stand at breakneck speed.

The judges had seen enough.

"Next contestant!" Barkle cried.

"That's us, sir," Stanley whispered to Applefeller.

"No! No!" Sweet yelled. "In respect of my King of Dessert status you *must* give me another chance."

"But Sweet," George Saucery said, "your dessert is a *moving* dessert. Next year, bring a *stationary* dessert and I'm sure you'll do much better!"

Sweet was stunned. The unnatural glossy shine on his face dimmed.

"Then help me chase the pies and stop them!" he begged.

"Fiddlefaddle!" declared George Saucery.

"Next contestant!" Barkle repeated. "Whoa! Hey! What's going on here?"

In a flash two of the roller-skating pies had skated under Barkle's feet, taking him for an unexpected tour of the dessert grounds. His long black robe waved wildly in the late afternoon breeze as he whooshed here and there, through a group of reporters and past Applefeller's apple pancake.

"Help! Stop these things!" Barkle cried. "I *hate* this dessert! Historically speaking, I would compare this dessert to a roller coaster!"

Boom! Barkle zigzagged into Reginald Coco's dessert table, scattering spoons, whipped cream, chocolate, and sprinkles over a group of surprised spectators.

"What a mess! All over my new suit!" yelled one man who had been especially splattered.

Smash! Barkle knocked against a table of nuts and hot fudge.

Policemen chased the judge around the field. Cameramen tried to keep him in focus. But that was getting harder every minute, for Barkle was moving faster and faster around the dessert grounds, destroying everything in his path.

Crash! Down fell an entire row of tables!

"Things are getting a bit out of hand down there," Stanley's father said, standing up.

"Oh hush, dear," his wife replied. "It's only Judge Barkle skating. Stanley can take care of himself."

"Better protect our flying apple pies, sirs!" Stanley cried to Applefeller and the Ragoon. "Judge Barkle is wrecking everything!"

"Yes! Yes! We must!" Applefeller yelled. "We still have to be judged!"

Applefeller, the Ragoon, and Stanley flew in high gear to their table.

"Hurry!" Applefeller cried. "He's heading right for us!"

Stanley and the Ragoon looked over their shoulders. Barkle was thundering closer.

"Oh no, sirs!" Stanley cried.

But then something absolutely incredible happened. The four flying pies trembled as though they knew they were in mortal danger, then began to bounce very quickly up and down. Just as Barkle was about to smash them to bits, they roared down the dessert table and soared into the air. Everyone in the dessert grounds blinked. Voices echoed up and down the field.

"It's a bird!"

"It's a plane!"

"It's a flying dessert!"

Over by the garage bins Josiah Benson shrieked in

166

delight: "I knew those pies would get airborne! I felt it in my whiskers!"

Applefeller grinned.

"Wow!" he yelled. "Ragoon! We did it!"

"Look!" Stanley cried. "They're flying in formation!"

The four pies, side by side, were making swooping figure eights above the dessert grounds. The crowd cheered.

"A most impressive dessert!" Hamilton Crusthardy exclaimed.

"Yes!" Brewster McLaughlin agreed. "After those pies land, I look forward to tasting them!"

The success of Applefeller's flying pies was making Sweet even more panicked.

"Please, please!" he begged the judges. "You must taste one of *my* pies!"

"Out of the question," said Hamilton Crusthardy.

"But you must!" Sweet exploded.

"But we cannot!" George Saucery yelled. "Your dessert has skated away!"

"Quite so!" Brewster McLaughlin remarked. "Now leave us! Pies are flying so it follows that we should watch!"

The pies were putting on quite a show—diving, turning, and twisting all around the stadium.

"They're flying backward!"

"They're flying frontward!"

"Sideways!"

"Upside down!!"

Meanwhile, Judge Barkle was still careering around the grounds. The popsicle stick on his caramel apple waved wildly in the wind.

"Help!" he cried. "Somebody please, please stop this dessert!"

Now Barkle was heading straight toward Josiah Benson's roped-off garbage area, stocked with forty large trash bins, each stuffed with half-eaten desserts, wrappers, crusts, and whipped cream. Josiah Benson was just putting the last trash bag into one of the bins when he saw Barkle racing toward him, reeling out of control, policemen and cameramen in pursuit.

"Stop me!" Barkle yelled.

"Don't mess up my trash!" Josiah Benson yelled back.

It was too late.

Barkle did a double backflip and landed face first in the largest, smelliest, messiest bin of garbage. The two roller-skating apple pies that had been under his feet sailed high into the air.

Sweet saw his last chance of getting one of his pies tasted.

"Tuba!" he barked.

In an instant Tuba's trunk snapped up, caught one of the pies, and handed it to Sweet.

"Good boy, Tuba!" he exclaimed. "You are the Prince of Pie Catchers!"

24 · Flying Apple Pies

SWEET SPOKE too soon. For Tuba had caught the pie with such a firm grip that he squashed it into a mash of little crumbs and still spinning roller skates. But Sweet—desperate, wild-eyed, willing to try anything—grabbed the pie and placed it on his table in front of the three remaining judges.

As the flying pies continued to dip and dive overhead, a squad of policemen was attempting to fish Barkle out of the garbage with a hastily mobilized crane. Josiah Benson backed away to join Applefeller, Stanley, and the Ragoon.

"What's this?" George Saucery said with disgust as he looked over Sweet's mangled pie.

"My dessert!" Sweet said.

"Your what?" Brewster McLaughlin said.

"Yes! My dessert!" Sweet repeated.

"But it's squashed!"

"Taste it anyway!" Sweet implored.

"No!" Brewster McLaughlin said. "I won't taste a squashed dessert. I may eat part of a roller skate and chip a tooth."

"But I'm the King of Dessert!"

169

"You are the king of nothing!" George Saucery snapped. "Our decision is quite final! No squashed desserts!"

Sweet's upper lip twitched.

Suddenly, the crowd started cheering:

"Flying pies! Flying pies!"

The sound rang in Sweet's ears and echoed through the nooks and crannies of his brain. His face turned deathly white. His orange tuxedo deoranged. He was the very picture of a defeated man. He looked skyward and moaned. For now the flying pies had sprouted short wings and were spinning in tight circles like tops. Then, suddenly, white smoke began to jet from the pies.

"Well, hush my puppies!" Josiah Benson exclaimed. "What are they doin' now?"

"They're writing something!" a policeman cried.

"What are they writing?" yelled a young girl.

"I can't tell yet!" said the policeman.

The dessert grounds grew so quiet you could hear an oven preheat as the flying pies swerved up and down writing a message. After a minute their bold white lettering spelled:

APPLE

After two minutes the words read:

APPLEFELLER HAS

Finally, after three minutes, the message was complete:

APPLEFELLER HAS HEART!

Josiah Benson jumped up and down.

170

"Well, cover me with roses and plant me in a garden!" he yelled. "No truer meanings have ever been written!"

Applefeller faced the Ragoon. The Ragoon grinned and shrugged.

"To make the pies a bit less sour
I added some Norwegian flour.
Siamese flour makes pies roll.
Norwegian flour makes them scroll."

Instantly, Applefeller and the Ragoon found themselves surrounded by a horde of dessert fans—the same fans who had insulted them an hour earlier. Small children asked for autographs and reporters demanded interviews.

"Applefeller, give it to me straight. Do any other of your desserts fly? Do any other of your desserts write? Could any of your desserts recommend any good movies?"

Everyone wanted to congratulate the creators of this exciting new dessert. After a while even Brewster McLaughlin, Hamilton Crusthardy, and George Saucery walked over and shook Applefeller's and the Ragoon's hands.

"A fine performance, Applefeller," George Saucery said.

"And by you, too, Captain Ragoon," Brewster McLaughlin said. "Josiah Benson and Stanley were right. You really can cook!"

"Yes!" Hamilton Crusthardy said as he watched the pies form a *V* over the judges' stand. "But what's most important is how they taste!"

The Ragoon nodded in agreement.

"As sweetly as our pies are flying—zipping through the sky—
You'll find, I think, that they taste *even sweeter than they fly."*

"And you'll get to taste 'em soon, I'd say," Josiah Benson said, noticing the pies flying closer and closer to the ground. "It looks like they want to land!"

"We'd better set up a runway, sir," Stanley suggested.

Applefeller, the Ragoon, Stanley, and Benson grabbed a long table and stood it on its four legs. As though they had radar, the pies gravitated toward the table, circling lower and lower. Everyone in the dessert grounds leaned forward and stood on tiptoes. One reporter went on the air: "I'm giving it to ya straight! Dessert contest history is being made today! Applefeller and the Ragoon's flying pies are going to land!"

But Sylvester Sweet had different ideas. The minute the words "Applefeller Has Heart" had appeared in the sky, something inside him snapped. He blinked and hit his head with his jeweled hand. His mustache twitched. Then a small cunning smile spread across his face and within seconds blossomed into a large sinister grin. Sweet

scanned the dessert grounds. The evil wheels in his brain began to turn so quickly you could see steam coming out of his ears. He started to laugh—an awful, hideous laugh halfway between a guffaw and a chortle that could only have come from a crazed, out of control, sick man.

Finally he took action.

"Tuuubbbbaaaaa!" he cried. *"Stop those flying pies!"*

25 · Crash Landings

WITH A sweep of his mighty trunk, Tuba lifted Sweet onto his back.

"Giddyap!" Sweet barked.

Tuba lurched into action, galloping in circles, lashing his trunk in the air like a whip.

"Get those pies, Tuba!" Sweet ordered. "Charge!"

"No!" Applefeller cried. "If the judges don't taste them, the pies can't win the contest!"

But Tuba was closing in, snapping his trunk back and forth, smashing everything in his way. The crowd dispersed, screaming. One reporter sent out an emergency broadcast. "Runaway elephant! Protect your desserts!"

"Things are getting dangerous," Stanley's father said. "I'm going down on the field to save my son."

"What?" his wife said, pulling her husband back into his seat. "And ruin Stanley's day? It's only an insane chef on an out-of-control elephant. Somebody will stop him— you'll see."

But who knew how to stop a rampaging elephant with a mad dessert chef on his back?

"I am the only King of Dessert!" Sweet cried.

Smash! Down went another row of dessert tables.

Bravely, Josiah Benson stood on the landing table and waved a bright red flag to guide the pies home. They swerved this way and that, trying to get close to the table and avoid Tuba at the same time. The pies flew left. Tuba darted after them. The pies flew around the judges' stand. Tuba barreled behind. Wherever the pies were, Tuba was there a fraction of a second later.

"Come on, pies!" cried a reporter. "You can do it!"

"Don't give up now!" yelled a policeman.

But you could see the pies were getting tired. They no longer turned corners as sharply. They stopped swerving with as much verve. Tuba, on the other hand, was picking up speed.

"Stop those pies!" Sweet bellowed.

Now everyone in the dessert grounds began cheering the pies on, chanting:

"Land! Land! Land! Land!"

"Hurry!" Applefeller cried.

A reporter screamed into his microphone: "The pies are fighting for their lives!"

"If those pies don't land in thirty seconds," Josiah Benson told Stanley, "it's all over!"

The pies aimed for the table and poured on every ounce of their remaining power.

"Go! Go! Go!"

"Come on!"

"Hurry!"

Small wheels suddenly appeared under the pies.

The Ragoon shouted:

"They're gonna make it! Never fear!
They're lowering their landing gear!"

The pies were twenty feet away from safety. The three

judges, with forks in hand, were waiting to taste them the second they landed.

Fifteen feet!

Ten feet!

"They're gonna make it!" Applefeller cried. "They're gonna make it!"

A roaring cheer filled the stadium.

"Yippee!"

"I love it!"

"All right!"

Then something awful happened. Tuba placed his right hoof directly into a giant piece of banana cream pie and started sliding straight toward the landing table.

"*No!*" Applefeller yelled.

But Tuba was traveling faster than any elephant has traveled before.

"It's gonna be close!" a reporter yelled. "It's gonna be close!"

The pies reached back inside their crusts and turned on every last bit of power they possessed. But Tuba was moving as fast as a cheetah.

"*Stop those pies!*" Sweet screamed.

Five feet!

The pies began to land. They were on the table. They were two feet away from the judges' forks!

Boooooooooooom!

Tuba smashed the flying pies off the table!

Squasssssshhhh! Tuba crushed all four flying pies!

"Good boy, Tuba!" Sweet cried as Tuba slid on past. "You are the Sultan of Smashers!"

The crowd moaned. Applefeller ran to the pies, got down on his knees, and picked up part of a crumbling crust. It fell into little bits in his trembling fingers. He looked back over his shoulder at the Ragoon, Stanley, and Josiah Benson, with teary eyes and quivering lips.

"They're totally destroyed!" he said. "Now the judges can't taste them! We can't win!"

The Ragoon, Stanley, and Josiah Benson were grimly silent. There was nothing to say. To make matters worse, Tuba hadn't stopped sliding on the piece of banana cream pie. In fact, still demolishing everything in his path, he circled around the field and was now heading right for the judges! McLaughlin, Crusthardy, and Saucery tried to run out of the way, but their black gowns got tangled and they fell in a heap directly in Tuba's path.

"He'll crush my powerful jaw!" Crusthardy moaned.

"My belly will protect us!" Brewster McLaughlin yelled.

Sweet was laughing wildly.

"Get them, Tuba!" he cried. "Don't stop!"

Tuba couldn't have stopped if he'd wanted to. He thundered forward as though he'd been shot from a cannon onto a sheet of ice.

"Noooooooo!" the judges yelled.

"I am the King of Dessert!" Sweet cried.

"The judges are goners!" yelled a reporter. "The judges are goners!"

"I'm too smart to be done in by an elephant!" George Saucery cried.

Tuba was only ten feet away . . .

Five feet . . .

Three . . .

"Good-bye, sweet sugar!" Brewster McLaughlin wailed.

But then, when Tuba was half a second away from steamrolling the judges flatter than crepes Suzettes, a hairy leg shot out and tripped him. With a thunderous honk Tuba flew into the air. Sweet held on for dear life as the elephant did a triple somersault over the three judges.

Sweet's face was green. "Bad Bishop of Beasts," he moaned. "Put me down!"

But Tuba was far from down himself. Around and around he flew, spinning wildly, his four legs flailing in four different directons until, finally, his body straightened out and he began to fall to earth like a rock.

"*Tuuuuubbbbbaaaaaaa!*" Sweet cried.

"Clear the area!" yelled a policeman. "He's going to land!"

The crowd scattered.

Bammmm!

With a weighty crash, Tuba fell—smack in the middle of Applefeller's apple-pancake trampoline.

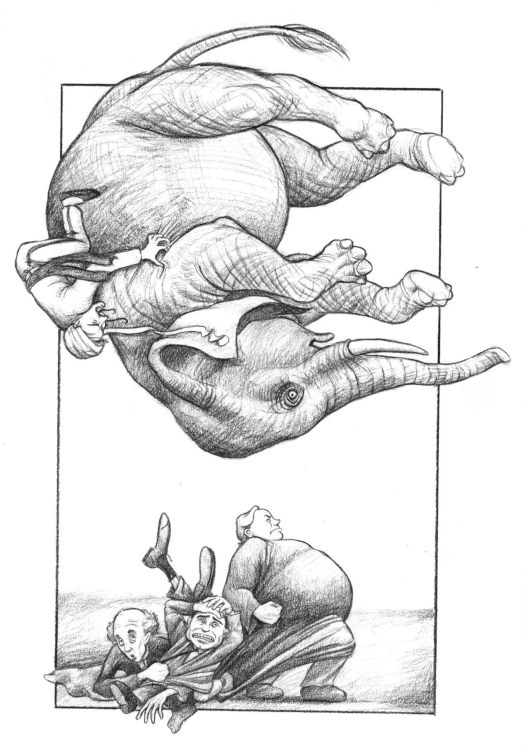

179

Bounce! Up they sailed, Tuba and Sweet! Then down. Then up again. If the fat Brewster McLaughlin bounced high, you can imagine how high a two-ton elephant went— well over three hundred feet.

The dessert grounds were safe again. Policemen circled the pancake, waiting to arrest Sweet and Tuba once they stopped bouncing.

Judges McLaughlin, Crusthardy, and Saucery stood up slowly, shaking with relief.

"That was close," George Saucery said as he wiped off his black gown. "I thought I was on my way to those great dessert grounds in the sky."

"And I thought I had tasted my last cake!" Hamilton Crusthardy added.

"But who tripped Tuba?" Brewster McLaughlin asked.

"Only the best animal on four legs," Josiah Benson declared.

Next to him stood Morocco, happily eating a carrot out of Stanley's hand.

26 · Just Desserts

As Tuba and Sweet were flipping onto Applefeller's pancake, Judge Barkle was being lifted by the crane out of his large bin of garbage. Twelve policemen were waiting there (holding their noses) with towels to wipe him off. But before they could offer any assistance, Barkle stormed away toward the other judges, his face crimson with anger. Bits of ice cream wrappings, soggy cake, eclairs, and strawberry sauce fell off his body as he moved through the crowd. His caramel apple was completely covered with lemon meringue.

But when Barkle reached his fellow judges, he did not break stride. Instead, he picked up his pace and headed straight for John Applefeller. Barkle looked him squarely in the eye.

"Yes sir?" Applefeller said haltingly.

"I hold *you*, Applefeller, personally responsible for what just happened to me *and* to the dessert grounds!"

Barkle was so angry he had trouble getting the words out.

"But sir, I didn't . . ."

"I know Sweet made the roller-skating apple pies that dumped me in the garbage, but it reeks of Applefeller, Applefeller and more *Applefeller*! This is it! The last straw! I told you that if I got hurt in any way I was holding you responsible, and I meant it! I'm throwing you out! *Out! Out! Forever!*"

Applefeller was so shocked he couldn't speak.

"Hoppin' hogtoads! You can't do that!" Josiah Benson said.

"Watch me," Barkle said.

"The skating pies wouldn't halt.
Why's that Applefeller's fault?"

the Ragoon asked.

"Because I say so," Barkle exclaimed. "And what I say so *is* so!"

"But Sweet destroyed our flying apple pies before they could be tasted! You have to give us a chance next year!" Applefeller said.

"Nothing doing, Applefeller," Judge Barkle said.

"But that means I can never enter again!" Applefeller said.

"Tough cookies," Barkle replied.

"You're a lousy man!" Stanley said.

"Silence!" Barkle barked. "I have spoken."

Judge Barkle walked back to be with his three companions before the sudden-death dessert taste-off between Michel Deserts and Reginald Coco.

Applefeller slumped down on his tree stump. People throughout the dessert grounds looked at him sympathetically. Then Stanley got an idea. He took Josiah Benson and the Ragoon aside and whispered something to them.

"Well then," Barkle said, trying to regain his composure and look dignified even though he was covered with trash, "the rules of the sudden-death dessert taste-off are as follows. Each contestant will . . ."

"Wait!"

The judges turned their heads to face the voice. It was Stanley. Barkle met his eyes with a disgusted scowl.

"Oh no! Not you again!" he moaned. "What do you want?"

"You have to judge our dessert."

Applefeller stared blankly after Stanley.

"What's going on here, Stanley?" he began, rising to his feet. "Our flying pies were destroyed. We all saw it. We have no dessert."

"But we *do* have a dessert, sir," Stanley said.

"We do?" Applefeller asked.

"Yes! Yes! The pie that you made for lunch! We haven't eaten it yet!"

"We can't enter that old thing!" Applefeller said. "It's only a simple apple pie!"

"Go ahead, Johnny! It'll do well," Josiah Benson said.

"A simple, tasty apple pie.
Go ahead and give a try!"

the Ragoon said as he took the pie out of the lunch pail.

Nathaniel Barkle glowered.

"I'm not touching that thing, let alone tasting it," he said. "I've been through enough for one day!"

"But you've got to," Josiah Benson exclaimed. "If not,

you'll be disobeyin' the Dessert Constitution which you wrote yourself. And if I registered your ink correctly, volume four, section three, letter E, page forty-nine, paragraph seventy-five, says: All contestants must be judged!"

The Ragoon stepped forward:

"Won't you let me clarify?
Eat your words—or eat this pie!"

"Over my dead body!" Judge Barkle exclaimed.

"No, wait a second here. They're right," Brewster McLaughlin broke in. "We must taste this dessert. The Dessert Constitution insists upon it! Also, considering how entertaining Applefeller and the Ragoon's flying pies were, we owe it to them to give Applefeller a chance, even if it's with a dessert that's doomed to lose. . . . But let's make it quick, shall we? It's almost suppertime. You taste first, Nathaniel."

George Saucery took the apple pie from the Ragoon and handed it to Barkle. Without pausing a second, Barkle handed the dessert directly to Brewster McLaughlin.

"I'm not going to taste that thing!" he declared. "It'll hurt me! I know it!"

"Come, come, Nathaniel!" Hamilton Crusthardy said. "Stop whimpering!"

"No!"

The three judges looked disapprovingly at Barkle. Finally, Brewster McLaughlin patted his enormous belly and took out his fork. "OK, OK. I'll taste first."

"But this is not fair!" Michel Deserts cried, twirling his cane violently.

"Quiet, Deserts!" McLaughlin broke in. "Certainly you are not scared of losing to an apple pie?"

Deserts frowned, but stepped back. Only a handful of the spectators and reporters left after Tuba's rampage bothered to look to see how Applefeller's simple dessert would be judged. After the thrill of Applefeller's flying apple pies, an apple pie that didn't promise to do anything held no appeal.

McLaughlin cut a large piece and then looked over his shoulder at Tuba and Sweet, still bouncing up and down on the pancake.

"I hope this pie turns into a toy too!" he said.

Applefeller stood by, looking miserable. McLaughlin waved the piece of pie under his nose and breathed deeply. "Hmm . . . it's actually highly aromatic for such an unremarkable dessert."

Then he put the fork in his mouth.

"Hmmm," he exclaimed. "It's good! The blend of sugars is highly excellent."

He swallowed and rubbed his belly.

"Applefeller," he said, "you've redefined the ordinary. A fine dessert! Here Hamilton, take a bite!"

Stanley smiled confidently at the Ragoon. Josiah Benson scratched his beard and then crossed his fingers.

Crusthardy flexed his mighty jaw four times and took out his fork. He cut into the pie and brought the piece close to his eye.

"Interesting color," he said. "Light brown, yet off-maroon."

He put the pie in his mouth.

"*Ahhhh! Ahhhhhhhhhhhhhhhhhhhhhh!* This crust is very fine! What an exciting taste. This dessert may not skate or fly, but that's no matter. Applefeller, you've made the usual unusual. Frankly, I'm charmed. Come, come, George. Take a bite."

George Saucery approached the dessert, fork in hand, and took a bite.

"Hmmm . . ." he scowled, "I don't taste any ice cream, but in a pie, that's acceptable."

Saucery licked his fork and after a second allowed himself a small grin.

"This dessert is simple, yet not simpleminded. We've placed much emphasis lately on the new-fangled dessert. But this pie demonstrates the importance of the old-fangled dessert. I like that. Here it is Nathaniel, you try."

Barkle hesitated and then spoke in a low, controlled voice. *"I won't taste that man's dessert!"*

"Come now. It's perfectly safe," George Saucery said. "In fact, it's so unusually delicious that I'm tempted to hand Mr. Applefeller the Silver Spoon right now!"

Michel Deserts had to be held back by two policemen.

Reginald and Razine meditated fervently in an effort to maintain their self-control. Applefeller stood up straight, a small smile on his lips. Maybe his chances hadn't ended when Tuba destroyed the flying pies. Morocco reared and did a little two-step on her hind legs. . . . Meanwhile, Tuba and Sweet had just taken their last bounce on the trampoline and were now being read their rights by the squad of policemen.

"*I won't taste that man's dessert!*" Barkle cried.

"Oh, come on!" Brewster McLaughlin said. "If you don't taste it we can't give out the Silver Spoon. It's late and I want to get a few bounces in on Applefeller's pancake before it gets too dark! Now be a good sport."

"*No!*"

"OK, Nathaniel!" McLaughlin said. "You've asked for it! *Police!*"

Three policemen grabbed Barkle by the arms and shoulders and held him firmly in place.

"*No!*" Barkle cried, kicking and clawing. But he was outnumbered. As McLaughlin and Crusthardy held Barkle's mouth open, George Saucery cut a piece of the pie and put it on his tongue. Then the three policemen, McLaughlin, and Crusthardy lifted him into the air and shook him up and down, forcing him to chew. Barkle struggled, but the grip on him was too strong. He kept chewing. And after he had chewed a while, he swallowed. And it was then that his expresson changed.

His brow wrinkled. His eyes narrowed. He stopped

kicking and clawing. McLaughlin, Crusthardy, and the policemen relaxed their grip and put him down. Barkle walked to the tree stump like a sleepwalker and sat down, lost in deep thought. For five minutes no one spoke as Barkle scanned the huge amount of dessert information he had stored away in his head. Every so often he licked his lips and scratched his chin. His caramel apple glimmered against the setting sun.

Finally, Barkle met Applefeller's eyes and spoke in a quiet voice.

"This dessert is wonderful! Historically speaking, I would compare this apple pie to the apple pie eaten by Moses before receiving the Ten Commandments."

Everyone gasped. One lady fainted, for this was the highest praise *any* dessert had ever received.

"*Non!*" Michel Deserts yelled. "It cannot be so good as that! *C'est impossible!*"

"It is possible, Deserts," George Saucery said. "Your dessert was good, but Applefeller's is better. Next year, bring a better dessert and I'm sure that you'll do better!"

"*Non!*" Deserts cried. "But I come so close!"

"Tough luck, Deserts. You lose," Brewster McLaughlin said. "The winner of the Silver Spoon is John Applefeller."

Applefeller nearly collapsed and fell over backward. He couldn't believe it was true. Stanley, the Ragoon, and Josiah Benson, the only people who believed in him all along, smiled happily.

"It's wonderful, sir."

"As great as a herd of leapin cowdogs!"

*"It's very true that no one's sweller
Than good old Johnny Applefeller."*

the Ragoon chirped with a small click of his heels. The crowd smiled and applauded. Reporters snapped Applefeller's picture and lined up for interviews. The judges shook his hand.

But Michel Deserts started screaming and running around in circles. Reginald Coco and Razine began shouting a prayer. Hamilton Crusthardy motioned for another squad of policemen.

"We don't want any more trouble," he said. "Get them out of here!"

As Deserts, Coco, and Razine were being escorted from the field, Judge Barkle turned to Applefeller and said, "I never thought I'd be saying this, but that was a fine dessert!"

"What were the ingredients?" Crusthardy inquired.

"Well," Applefeller began, "nothing special. Only fresh apples, flour, cinnamon, butter, and sugar."

"You mean there was no scissors sugar?" Brewster McLaughlin said. "I could have sworn I tasted scissors sugar!"

"No," Applefeller admitted. "Only white and brown sugar."

"And heart," murmured Josiah Benson, winking at Stanley.

"And now," Nathaniel Barkle announced, "we must present the prize to John Applefeller!"

27 · The Caramel Apple

JUDGE BARKLE took the Silver Spoon from his pocket.

"I present to you, John Applefeller . . ."

Just then, Sweet stumbled by on his way to the stationhouse, held by four policemen.

"Hey, Applefeller," he said, interrupting Barkle, "you dessert nobody . . ."

"He's no dessert nobody now, Sweet!" Josiah Benson said. "You are! he just won himself the Silver Spoon."

"Applefeller?" Sweet muttered. "I thought Michel Deserts and Reginald Coco were to have a taste-off."

"Yes, me!" Applefeller said.

"But I am the King of Dessert!" Sweet cried.

"No, no, no!" Brewster McLaughlin said. "Applefeller is this year's King of Dessert. You are soon to be the King of the Jailbirds for destroying the dessert grounds. Now get away. You're ruining the Silver Spoon ceremony!"

"But what was your dessert?" Sweet asked. "I was sure I destroyed your flying pies."

"An apple pie!" Applefeller beamed.

"An apple pie?" Sweet said. "An apple . . ." He stopped midsentence, then faced the judges with a broad smile. They eyed him suspiciously.

"If I am to give up my King of Desserts status," Sweet began, "it's only fair that I should be able to taste the dessert that has de-desserted me."

"You want to taste *my* dessert?" Applefeller said in disbelief.

"Yes, I do, Mr. Applefeller," Sweet said, "for I have always deeply appreciated your dessert techniques."

"Dancin' hogpuppies you have!" Josiah Benson squeaked.

And the Ragoon added:

"Sweet is laying it on thick.
Don't believe him. It's a trick!"

"Yes sir," Stanley agreed.

"How could it possibly be a trick?" Sweet said, apparently taken aback. "After all, I have already lost the Silver Spoon."

"Quite so!" said Hamilton Crusthardy.

"Indeed!" George Saucery said. "I think Sweet should taste a good simple dessert."

"Thank you, sir," Sweet said.

"Hand me the pie, will you, Stanley?" Applefeller asked.

"Right away, sir."

Stanley went to Applefeller's table, picked up the pie, and brought it to Sylvester Sweet.

Sweet smiled and nodded. After checking his hair in the diamond ring on the fourth finger of his left hand, he took the pie.

"Well, if you're going to taste the pie, it follows that you should hurry!" Brewster McLaughlin commented.

"Yes! Eat!" Nathaniel Barkle said.

Sweet looked at the dessert coyly.

"Yes! I, Sylvester S. Sweet, the ex-King of Dessert will now taste the new King of Dessert's dessert . . . over my dead body!"

192

Sweet gripped the pie firmly in his right hand and aimed straight for Applefeller's head. He threw with all his might.

"Duck, sir!"

Applefeller dropped to his knees, and the pie flew over him, smack into Nathaniel Barkle.

"What!" Barkle yelled, as apple pie dripped off of his face. "I knew it! I knew it! Oh, what a day! I *always* get hurt by Applefeller's desserts! I don't know how it happens, but it happens!"

Then, very quickly, Josiah Benson's arm snapped forward, and an apple whizzed through the air and smashed into Sweet's mouth. Sweet's hands shot up to his lips.

He grabbed at the apple and pulled. But no matter how hard he tried, he couldn't get the apple loose. It had stuck rock solid between his gums.

"Take that, Sweet!" Benson cried. "I've been wantin' to shut your trap for a cowdog's age!"

The Ragoon smiled.

"Sweet is a man who is horribly ruthless.
Now he is the one who is finally toothless!"

Judges McLaughlin, Saucery, and Crusthardy laughed.

"About time!" Brewster McLaughlin said.

"MMMMmmmmhhhMMM!" Sweet moaned as he tried, unsuccessfully, to pull the apple from his mouth.

"Get him out of here!" Hamilton Crusthardy demanded.

Sweet continued to moan and clutch at the apple as three policeman grabbed him and dragged him to the stationhouse.

But Judge Barkle was not thinking about Sweet. There was an apple pie smushed all over his face.

"Applefeller!" he said. "You are a disgrace! The moldly Oreo in the cookie jar of this contest!"

"Now, now, Nathaniel!" George Saucery interrupted. "Stop sputtering. You're not hurt—just a little pie on your face to go with the ice cream and cake on your body."

There was truth in George Saucery's words for Barkle

was so covered with dessert that he looked as though he should have been entering the contest instead of judging it.

Applefeller looked at Nathaniel Barkle in embarrassment.

"Can I help you wipe up?"

"*No!*" Barkle thundered. "I never want to see you in this contest again in my life! You've won your Silver Spoon, now get *out!*"

But the always helpful Stanley grabbed a towel, rushed to Barkle's side, and started to help him wipe off the apple pie.

"I can wipe my own face, thank you," Barkle exclaimed.

Barkle took the towel from Stanley.

"There! Much better!" he said.

Stanley gasped.

"And what are you looking at?" Barkle demanded.

Stanley closed and opened his eyes. He adjusted his glasses.

"Your . . . your apple, sir. It's dissolving!"

"What?"

"Unbelievable!"

"Really now!"

Everyone gathered around Barkle. He could barely breathe for all the people suddenly crowding him.

"Get away! Give me room!" he yelled.

Everyone took a step backward. Then Barkle slowly, nervously put his hand up to his face and felt his caramel apple. His fingers twitched as he gingerly touched the fruit that had plagued him for so long. But it was true! The apple had started to melt away!

"It's dissolving! It is!" Barkle announced happily. "I should have known Applefeller couldn't make a dessert that didn't eventually change into something else. This simple apple pie of yours is also a de-gluing agent!"

"Give it a pull, Nathaniel!" Brewster McLaughlin said.

Barkle grabbed the apple firmly in his hands and yanked as hard as he could. The apple came off with a loud pop.

"All right, Nathaniel!"

"Hooray!"

"Give me that apple!" one reporter cried. "We can display it in the Appleton Dessert Museum!"

Barkle handed over the apple and smiled broadly. He looked ten years younger. His wrinkles instantly un-wrinkled.

"Congratulations!" Applefeller said.

"I should still be angry with you, Applefeller," Barkle began. "But what the heck! Let's let bygones be bygones, shall we? Historically speaking, I would compare my apple to the apple that got stuck to Buddha's face before he entered Nirvana, and he didn't hold any grudges, so why should I?"

"Thank you, sir!" Applefeller beamed.

*"I think the time is opportune
To present the Silver Spoon."*

the Ragoon said.

"Yes, of course," Barkle chuckled. "I present this Silver Spoon to you John Applefeller for a delightfully delicious apple pie."

Applefeller took the spoon from Barkle.

"Thank you very much," he said.

Barkle turned toward the other three judges. "I'm so glad, I could taste a thousand more desserts right now!" he exclaimed.

"How about a bounce on Applefeller's pancake instead?" McLaughlin suggested with a wry smile.

Barkle paused and looked worried.

"Come on! It won't hurt you!" McLaughlin said. "Nothing serious happened to you last year. It's not at all scary if you relax and enjoy the ride."

"Count me in," Barkle said, "but only if Crusthardy comes along!"

"Oh no! Not me!" Hamilton Crusthardy said. "I might hurt my mighty mouth and ruin my career!"

"Hogwash, Hamilton!" Judge Barkle said. "What are you so scared of?"

"Me scared?" Hamilton Crusthardy countered. "I'm certainly not scared of a silly pancake! I'll go if Saucery agrees to take a bounce."

All eyes turned to a stern-looking George Saucery.

"Well . . . why not?" he conceded.

"Bravo!"

"Nicely done!"

"Let's go before it gets too dark!" Brewster Mc-Laughlin said. "Last one to the pancake is a carton of melted ice cream!"

28 · Going Home

APPLEFELLER LOOKED with great satisfaction at the four judges sprinting toward his pancake.

It had been a long day. Pies had skated and pies had flown, but after all the fireworks the best dessert of the year was the simplest.

Applefeller looked at the beautiful Silver Spoon in his right hand. He had never seen it up close before. He rubbed his thumb gently over the carved portrait of Zeus on the handle, working his way up to Thomas Jefferson writing the Declaration of Independence with one hand and eating a slice of pumpkin pie with the other, and finally to the delicate etching on the bowl of a boy and girl eating a hot fudge sundae. Morocco butted her head against Applefeller's right side and Applefeller stroked her mane.

Applefeller looked at Stanley.

"Winning feels good, doesn't it, sir?" Stanley said.

"Oh yes," Applefeller said, "but I still can't believe my pie won. I always thought that to do well in today's world one had to be as original as possible."

"Only for some folks," Josiah Benson said. "Take the Ragoon here. Now he speaks in rhymes, so for him it's normal to make crazy desserts. But you still journey by horse everywhere ya go. For you it's natural to be simple."

Applefeller looked at the Ragoon.

"You came all the way back from Iambia for nothing. Sweet stole your roller-skating pies and then destroyed your flying pies. And then I won the contest on my own."

The Ragoon smiled.

"I saw something else that was equally sweet,
Sylvester S. Sweet going down in defeat.
And what is much better than any award—
The integrity of all dessert is restored."

Morocco licked Applefeller's face. Behind him, Tuba and Dentina were being led off the field. The last camera crews were putting away their gear.

Just then Stanley's parents made their way across the dessert grounds.

"Hi, Mom and Dad," Stanley said.

"What a wonderful contest," his mother said.

"Yes," his father agreed. "All that action! I loved every minute!"

Applefeller shook Stanley's parents' hands and introduced the Ragoon and Josiah Benson.

"We've heard so much about you both," Stanley's mother said.

The Ragoon smiled:

"You've a extra special son.
Stanley here makes cooking fun!"

"That's as true as a herd of hoppin' toaddogs!" Josiah Benson agreed.

"Absolutely," Applefeller added.

"Our pleasure," Stanley's father replied, patting Stanley on the shoulder.

"Let's not stand here like gophers in a pigpen!" Josiah Benson said. "Let's go home and have us a celebration!"

"What a fine idea," Stanley's mother said. "Stanley, you can stay out as long as you want."

"What do ya mean?" Benson exclaimed. "You're comin' with us!"

"But we didn't do anything," Stanley's father said.

"I don't know about that," Josiah Benson said. "You raised Stanley, right? That's a cowdog of an achievement in and of itself!"

The Ragoon nodded and led Stanley's father toward the cart.

"You made his bed and sewed his shirts.
You made him grow to love desserts!"

"That's true," Stanley said. "Come on! It's already getting dark!"

Stanley hitched Morocco to the cart and they all climbed aboard. The first stars began to shine as they made their way out of the dessert stadium—three men, one boy, two parents, and their horse. Applefeller looked up into the sky and saw the faint gleaming of the Big Dipper. He rubbed the Silver Spoon in his right hand.

"Oh yes," he said, "we're going to have quite a celebration! Quite a celebration indeed!"

29 · Applogue

AFTER APPLEFELLER, other great dessert chefs were awarded the Silver Spoon. Michel Deserts won the next year with a simple chocolate crepe. Reginald Coco and Razine won the year after with a pineapple hot fudge sundae. Sadly, however, Princess Irma Frostina never placed higher than 510th. She spent her golden years in Germany in a home for deranged dessert chefs.

The police decided that once Sweet had spent a brief time in jail he should devote the rest of his life to community service. He became the new Worldwide Dessert Contest janitor—and a silent janitor at that. The apple Josiah Benson threw at him remained wedged in his mouth until his dying day. Luckily, a doctor was able to bore a hole through the middle of the apple so Sweet could eat by sucking in his food through a straw.

Like Sweet, Dentina was also put to work. She spent her time filing entry forms in the dessert registrar's office.

And Tuba paid his debt to society as well. Every year at the contest Tuba was employed giving rides to hundreds of happy children. After a few years there was no doubt in anyone's mind that Tuba was a completely reformed elephant.

The four judges continued their duties for years.

Nathaniel Barkle reached new heights in historical dessert research. By the time he retired Barkle could be heard saying: "Historically speaking, I would compare the taste of this chocolate ice cream to the chocolate ice cream Homer ate on the sixth day of the Trojan War." Indeed, Barkle's historical taste buds knew no limits.

And with no caramel apple attached to his face, Barkle began to enjoy life. In fact, free of that brown apple, Barkle was a handsome man. In his final years he split time between scholarly dessert pursuits and modeling for a stylish fashion magazine.

Judge Brewster McLaughlin continued to create new kinds of sugar (many of them unusable, like frog sugar and liver sugar). But at least five hundred of his more conventional brands (such as air sugar and clown sugar) found their way into kitchens around the world.

Hamilton Crusthardy built up his muscular mouth and jaw to a point so rarefied that he could tell not only the exact temperature and cooking time of a cake, but also the type of oven and spatula used.

As he grew older, George Saucery devoted more and more time to dessert research and wrote an internationally acclaimed thousand-page bestseller, "Ice Cream Is Best Stored at Temperatures Below Freezing—Part Two."

The four judges got together socially once or twice a year to relax and reminisce. One name that always came up in conversation was John Applefeller.

"Ah yes," Barkle would begin, feeling the spot where he used to wear the caramel apple, "historically speaking, Applefeller was our most unusual contestant."

"Quite!" Brewster McLaughlin agreed with a broad grin, thinking fondly of Applefeller's apple pancake.

"Indeed!" George Saucery exclaimed.

"Yes!" Hamilton Crusthardy concurred. "And what a delicious apple pie he made the year he won the contest!"

John Applefeller, Stanley, Josiah Benson, and even the Ragoon lived happily in Appleton for many years.

Josiah Benson set up a balloon-ride business. Twice a day he would take any willing passengers for a spin in Applefeller's apple-soufflé balloon.

The Ragoon was quickly recognized as a great dessert genius. His creations tasted so much better than any other chef's that he never entered the contest on his own. Instead, he joined Barkle, McLaughlin, Crusthardy, and Saucery as the fifth judge. In years to come dessert contestants grew used to hearing the Ragoon's rhymed criticism:

"I taste you've imported your yeast from the East
When yeast from the West is usually best.
In contrast, you've measured your sugars precisely.
They blend with the yeast from the East very nicely."

Applefeller and Stanley devoted their energies to an apple pie business. After the Ragoon showed him how to prevent his pies from turning into de-gluing agents, Applefeller's Apple Pies could be found in supermarkets across the country in bright red packages with Morocco's picture on their fronts. Applefeller finally made a good living and no longer had to support himself with his failed desserts (although the United States Olympic wrestling team lost every match for years once Applefeller stopped supplying them with French toast kneepads). But more important, his days as a laughing stock were over. He became a respected member of the community. Every summer at The Worldwide Dessert Contest, Applefeller, Stanley, and Josiah Benson were given a front row box seat to watch the Ragoon judge.

And so the contest continued for years and years. If you ever visit Appleton maybe you can take a balloon ride with Josiah Benson, or taste one of Applefeller's pies, or bounce on the great apple pancake with Brewster McLaughlin, or talk in rhymes with the Ragoon, or see Judge Barkle's caramel apple on display at the Appleton Dessert Museum.

For as John Applefeller's Aunt Harriet used to say: *The importance of desserts must never be underestimated.*